For a few long ... **kissed her an** ... **back, Tessa forgot everything.**

She felt what she'd always felt around Griff, right down through her body—delightful, sensual desire. And she basked in the feeling of being close to a man she had once loved more than anyone else in the whole world.

Loved. Past tense.

The thought brought her back to reality, and she jerked away from him, stiffening.

"You shouldn't have done that," she said, staring at him.

"Why?" he asked quietly. "Because you liked it so much it's giving you second thoughts about what you're getting into? Because you're worried that the yearning you just felt is the way you're supposed to feel about the man you're marrying—plus a whole lot more?"

Hayley Gardner used to sit in her school history class while the teachers taught and write romances in her notebook instead of notes. That turned out just fine, because she could always study the textbooks and the teachers thought she was a most conscientious student who took down every word they said! Now, years later, she is thrilled to be following her dream of full-time writing—when she isn't home-schooling her son, that is. Any free time Hayley has is spent with her husband, or researching methods of teaching children with autism, or collecting dolls, or knitting, or taking long, deep breaths…and hoping her readers enjoy her efforts to make them smile and feel good about love.

KIDNAPPING
HIS BRIDE

BY
HAYLEY GARDNER

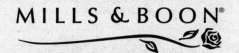

MILLS & BOON®

To all the people in Claiborne Parish who have gone out of their way to accept us,
help us and make us feel like family: because of you, living in Athens
is like living in Paradise.
Thank you.

And to Tina, Mary-Theresa, Miss Jeri Buckner and Sheriff Kenneth Volentine:
my heartfelt thanks for your help and/or expertise.

*First published in Great Britain 2003
Harlequin Mills & Boon Limited,
Eton House, 18-24 Paradise Road, Richmond, Surrey TW9 1SR*

© Florence Moyer 2002

ISBN 0 263 83337 2

*Set in Times Roman 10½ on 12 pt.
01-1103-47853*

*Printed and bound in Spain
by Litografía Rosés, S.A., Barcelona*

Chapter One

She was doing the right thing, Tessa Blake reassured herself as she paced in the foyer of one of Claiborne Landing's only two churches. In her white satin, pearl-studded, wedding dress, she was the bride-to-be she'd dreamed of being for almost all of her twenty-seven years—so what if she was marrying the wrong groom? There was nothing wrong with Clay Ledoux. Nothing at all. Had she been anyone but who she was, with any other past than the one she had, and had he been anyone else but who he was, she might have fallen hard for Clay. Even though she hadn't, this marriage was what she wanted, and nothing was going to stand in her way.

Through the closed door to the sanctuary, she could hear her grandmother, Sadie, who had taken her in when she'd been more or less orphaned at age twelve, playing the opening notes of the next to the last song before the "Wedding March." Focus. She needed to focus. So she concentrated on the music, and how happy she would be—

"Was leaving me off the invitation list my brother's idea—or yours?"

Not having heard the front door to the church brush open over the carpet behind her, Tessa jumped at the voice. Realizing whom it belonged to, she whirled around with a little gasp, her petticoats and satin skirt rustling back into place as she met the gaze of the man who had once played the leading role in all her dreams of being a bride. Griff. Clay's brother. Her former fiancé. She'd ended their engagement years before when she'd finally figured out that he'd be happier flying planes in the Air Force than stuck here in Claiborne Landing with her. To see him here, now, was totally unexpected, as was the physical attraction that slammed right into her stomach and edged down to her knees, making them weak. Exasperated that she could still feel anything for him, even physically, after having gone on with her life, she mustered up some gumption.

"For years on end you don't come home, and you expected an invitation?" she asked, purposely keeping her voice low so no one would come see whom she was talking to. "We figured you'd send your regrets. That you'd already be busy climbing in some pyramid. Or maybe flying off to see an ancient Greek ruin or some French art museum. Don't tell me you're calling a halt to your traveling before seeing all the Seven Wonders of the World?"

"Maybe," he drawled out, "I figured seeing Tessa Blake getting married without love, and to my brother, might qualify as the Eighth. At least, you got me wondering."

"How did you know that?" As soon as the sentence

was out of her mouth, she realized she'd just about verified the "marrying without love" part. It figured. She could never hide anything from Griff. That's why she tried to avoid him whenever he was in town for a visit. Mostly it had worked, except for that one time two years ago when she'd run into him, and spoken up when she shouldn't have. But she didn't want to dwell on the past.

"Someone told you about the wedding and that I wasn't in love?" she asked.

"And more, via e-mail."

More? She gulped. Already panicked, she was now feeling almost light-headed. "What more?"

He shrugged his broad shoulders. "Not important."

Not important to *him* maybe. Tessa took a slow, deep breath and tried to relax. If Griff knew the worst, he would not be that nonchalant.

"Who was this e-mail from?"

"I honestly don't know. The address was Please-Come@freebies.com." The muscle in his jaw throbbed. "You didn't send it, did you?"

"No!"

He believed her; she could tell by his solemn look.

"None of that is important right now," he said. "What is, is that you don't make the mistake of your life by walking down that aisle." He took a step closer to her, and Tessa backed up until she was almost at the still-closed door to the sanctuary. The last thing she wanted on the day she was getting married was to be this close to Griff. Even though her brain had written him a goodbye letter after he'd made her heart freeze up, it was like she'd forgotten to send a copy to the rest of her body. They hadn't been this close for years.

So many years.

"You have to leave," she said with as much authority as she could muster, not about to get into what kind of mistake she was about to make—or not. "I'm going to be getting married in about two minutes."

"So you say." Griff stared solemnly around the foyer, at the small, antique bookcase to one side and at the steep stairwell leading up to the classroom where they'd had Sunday School classes as children. "There's no one here to walk you down the aisle and give you away. Want me to?"

"No, Griff. You're the past. My future is on the other side of this door, and that's where I'm going. Alone."

He lifted his fingertips, brushed back a ringlet at her temple and then slid them slowly down the curve of her cheek, sending a shiver through her. "You swore to me a couple of years back you were going to have your dream, Tessa," he reminded her, his voice getting under her skin and reaching into her heart. "I'm here to make sure you don't give up on it."

Her dream? Then she remembered. The last time they'd really talked, during one of his rare visits "home," Griff had asked her why she'd never gotten married. She'd told him she wouldn't, not unless she fell in love, and that hadn't happened yet. That just as Griff had given up everything, including her, to pursue his dream, she was determined to have hers of a loving husband and children. The perfect family she'd never had, in the perfect home and hometown she hadn't had until her father had abandoned her, her mother had died, and the authorities had finally found Sadie. Griff was here to make sure she didn't give up on that dream. But how could he do that? They were through.

"You walked away years ago, remember?" she

asked. Her heart, already beating swiftly, pounded at his nearness. The woodsy scent he was wearing began to penetrate her defenses and cloud her thoughts. "You shouldn't care at this point."

"I shouldn't care," he agreed, his eyes never leaving her, "but I know how much pain a loveless marriage can cause—for both sides. I don't want you, or my brother, to have to go through that. And then there's—" Suddenly he shook his head. "No, there isn't time to get into that. Just postpone the wedding, and let's go talk."

"I can't," she said, shaking her head, wanting to ask him what there was no time to get into, but doing so would be pointless. "I'm marrying your brother, now. We can talk later."

"We need to talk now."

Of all the nerve... Behind her, "The Wedding March" started. Ready to enter the sanctuary and walk down the aisle, Tessa purposefully slid to Griff's side and began to turn toward the door. But before she could so much as put her hand on the golden knob, Griff swept her off her feet and hoisted her onto his shoulder. Pivoting, he headed through the still-open front door and down the brick steps of the church.

"Are you crazy?" Tessa asked breathlessly, batting his chest. He didn't respond. She swung her head from side to side, looking for help, but then she remembered the entire population of Claiborne Landing, all one hundred fifty-five of them, were stuffed into the church, courtesy of her grandmother. There wasn't so much as one old man idling his time away on the bench in front of the car repair shop across the road. Through the closed windows, with the noisy wall unit air conditioners humming and "The Wedding March" being played loudly, Tessa doubted anyone could hear her if she yelled for help. At least, she thought wryly, she didn't have to worry about the embarrassment of it all.

In the seconds it took to reach his shiny, silver-blue truck parked on the edge of the road, she was beyond the shock she'd experienced in the church, past the physical attraction, and all the way up to irritated. Very. He plopped her onto the driver's side seat, and she caught the breath that being thrown over his shoulder and bouncing the dozen yards had knocked loose from her. "What in the world do you think you are doing?"

"We're fixing to have a talk."

"You always did insist on having everything your way, didn't you?"

"If I had, darlin', you'd have married me when I graduated the Academy and come with me all over the world, and I'd have been toting you off to celebrate our wedding anniversary this month. But that's water under the bridge, isn't it?"

"Definitely." She gave her head an emphatic nod. "In fact, as far as I'm concerned, that bridge just crosses a dusty, dried out, old creek bottom now."

Griff's mouth twisted, and his ink-blue eyes scolded her. "All I'm trying to do is keep you—and my brother—from making a mistake."

"Like you and I made?"

"A mistake? Yeah, sure." He gave her another long look. "I'm good at making those." Then, to her embarrassment, he put one hand on her bottom and started to push her toward the passenger side. He didn't have to expend a lot of effort; the second his hand touched her, Tessa bolted right as though she'd been zapped with electricity.

Griff slid in beside her and shut the door.

"The sheriff is probably investigating right now why I'm not walking down the aisle. Kidnapping me is not a good idea, Griff. I could have you arrested."

The grin that was uniquely Griff's appeared as the truck roared to life, and they pulled out onto the narrow country road. She hadn't seen that grin for years, not since before the two of them had broken up. It was half-curved and kind of devilishly appealing, and it still had the power to melt her heart.

"Yeah," he agreed, "you could. But you won't. Getting me arrested would keep me in town a long time, wouldn't it? I'd be around to interfere in your plans."

He had a point. Griff, in town, was something she definitely did not desire.

"Besides, you don't want your wedding day to be a scandal the whole town talks about for years, do you?"

No, she didn't. It was already half-ruined, of course, and if Griff got his way, it would be totally shot, but it wasn't a scandal—not yet. She could still keep her personal business from becoming a tasty morsel for the town to munch on.

He rounded a corner carefully, heading away from the church down Highway 518 toward Athens, away from Claiborne Landing. Leaving town was something he was really good at, she thought bitterly, and then she wondered why she was giving him that much energy. She was over him.

"You're making a mistake, Tessa."

"The mistake being marrying your brother?" Tessa asked, her chin matching his for stubbornness. With great care, she kept herself from examining every inch of him with hungry eyes. She *was* marrying Clay as soon as she could get loose from Griff, and it wouldn't be right looking at another man.

He shook his head. "The mistake being not marrying for love. Did you really think for one minute that I wouldn't try to stop you from doing that?"

"Did you really think for one second that you'd have anything at all to say about it?"

"No," he admitted quietly. "But I'd like to. I'm an expert on why you shouldn't marry without love."

She remained silent, which was not what Griff had expected, because before, she'd always had a comment or opinion about *everything*. And so, being careful to check the roller coaster hills for oncoming traffic first, he ventured another look at her to see if he could tell what she was thinking.

When he'd thrown her over his shoulder and carried her out of the church, apparently he'd caused her veil to tilt. Her topknot was tipped, and curls from her long, ash-blond hair were now tumbling down around her temples. Even a little bedraggled, she was still the prettiest thing he'd ever laid eyes on, and still the most desirable woman he'd ever met. The years of being without her hadn't changed that.

Tessa took a deep breath, which got his attention. "So tell me about this e-mail."

"It came three days ago and mentioned all the particulars of the wedding—when, where, and whom—and then asked me to come stop it so you didn't end up marrying someone you didn't love." The other thing it had said, he didn't want to get into with her yet. Maybe not even ever.

"And you came, even though it's been over between us a long time?" Tessa didn't want to think about what that might mean.

"Like I said, I know what it is to marry someone you don't love, and go through the agony of a divorce. I'm sure you heard Janie and I—"

"Yes, I heard." She didn't want to discuss his former marriage with him. Talk about *pain*.

"I wasn't only thinking of you, you know, when I pulled you out of there. My brother's mixed up in this mess."

"With how little you've been back to see your family since you left home, I'm surprised you're that worried about Clay. You needn't be. His heart is safe with me."

"Mine wasn't."

"The broken heart worked both ways, Griff." She worked her teeth over her bottom lip, her slim shoulders stiffening with the memories under satin sleeves. "But Clay and I won't divorce. I'm positive of that."

"You were positive we would get married when I got my commission, too, and look at what happened."

The situations were totally different, but Tessa wasn't about to get into that. There was nothing else she could say without telling him a whole lot more than she was willing to.

"This is getting us nowhere." Removing her lacy gloves, she reached up and started to pull out the hairpins that were now, thanks to him, tangling up her carefully done hair. "We need to get whatever your problem is settled and me back to the wedding. So tell me what you want."

There was a long silence in the truck, and the air was heavy between them. "I want you to reconsider marrying Clay. I want you to find a man who will make you happy."

"I had one of those once, and he left town," she pointed out.

He winced. She didn't want him hurt, Tessa thought, but really, why was he here? She couldn't believe he had come home merely to "rescue" her—what was the point? He didn't want her. And how had he been able to get off on short notice anyway? Then she remembered. Six years he'd promised the Air Force for sending him to college. And those six years were up this month. June.

Her breath caught. "Are you home to stay, or planning to reenlist?" She was afraid to hear the answer; afraid to hear he'd changed his mind about the excitement he could experience "out there." If he stayed in Claiborne Landing, what on earth was she going to do, because she was still marrying Clay.

She had to.

"At this point, reenlist. I had vacation days coming, so I took them."

Relieved, Tessa kept her eyes averted and didn't answer, too afraid that if she looked at him or spoke, he would sense the fear she felt that he would stay...and the worry she felt that if he did go, she would never see him again. Never have that thrill course through her that she got whenever she looked at him, never—

But she would be married to someone else, so maybe it would be better if she never.

He steered skillfully around a curve as the roller coaster road turned into more of a snake, and she braced one white pump against the floor to keep from sliding toward the middle and touching him. She caught the movement of his head and looked at him, and that jolt came one more time, the one that said that somehow, she had to get him to leave town as fast as possible, or she could very well say or do something that could ruin the precarious happiness she'd fought so hard for in the years since he'd left.

With a long sigh, she put her hairpins she'd been gripping in the cup holder on his dashboard and took her veil off, carefully folding and smoothing it out on her lap. "Where are we going?"

"Someplace to talk. Not your house. That's the first place people would think of to look. Casey's Kitchen still open this time of day?"

She nodded. Casey's Kitchen was a cozy restaurant underneath a bunch of shady oaks on a well traveled highway that bisected Claiborne Landing. Its owner, Doc Casey, was a retired doctor in his sixties who had always claimed to love cooking more than doctoring, even though he'd been tremendously successful at medicine. He was also Tessa and her grandmother's best customer at the bakery they owned, buying sweets for his customers, which included lunch and dinner crowds of mostly truck drivers, farmers, ranchers and an occasional mom and small children out for a break. By two any afternoon, the place was usually deserted, and Tessa was happy to see from the empty parking lot that today was no different.

Before she got out of the truck, she laid her gloves and the veil on the console between the seats, and then fixed her hair and makeup as best she could in the tiny mirror on the visor. By the time she finished, Griff had come around and opened the truck door on her side, and was waiting there to help her down.

As his hands touched her waist, an involuntary wave of desire went through her, as well as a glimpse back into the past when she'd loved his touching her. But whatever she'd felt then wasn't important now. Griff didn't say a word, but by the impenetrable look on his face, she would guess he wasn't affected at all by touching her. That was all right. She didn't want to have to deal with Griff wanting her.

Doc Casey himself was behind the counter when she walked in, and Tessa nodded at him as though nothing at all were out of the ordinary and she wasn't attired in a white satin wedding dress. Trusting Griff would follow her, she went into the larger side room and settled at a small, relatively private table far to the rear of the place, hoping she was less noticeable back there. Griff sat down, too, close enough that their shoulders touched. She gave him a pursed mouth, questioning stare.

"If I sit on the other side of the table, I'll have to talk louder," he said, his voice low. She realized he was right and let him stay where he was, wishing she didn't feel like a quivering mass of emotions just because he was home.

Back, she corrected silently. Griff didn't want this to be home. He'd made that clear a long time ago.

Within seconds, Doc Casey came to take their order, his mirth-filled, green eyes gazing down at her from his round Irish face. "Griff. Welcome home. *Welcome.* Tessa, aren't you a little too fancied up for this place?"

"You have a dress down code?" Tessa lifted both hands into the air in a plea for him to spare her.

"It's my fault," Griff said, leaning back in his chair to look up at the former doctor. "I kidnapped her from her wedding."

"That so?" Doc Casey gazed down at Tessa with the same concerned, yet detached, expression he'd always used whenever she'd described her sneezes and sniffles.

"Plopped her right over my shoulder and carried her out kicking and screaming. Wanted to play a trick on my brother."

Although he was exaggerating, his excuse for her being here, having a private meal with her fiancé's brother when she was supposed to be at her wedding, was as good as any Tessa could make up. She glanced at Griff, and he winked, making her realize that saving her from having to give any explanation to Casey herself was exactly what he'd intended. His thoughtfulness caught her off balance.

"You haven't changed a mite," Doc Casey said, looking as if he wanted to laugh. "It was always you who did the hell-raising, and your brother who calmed everyone down."

"Oh, I think Clay will probably do some hell-raising when he gets here," Griff told him affably, as though he wasn't worried a bit.

Casey let out a loud chuckle. "Ain't that the truth, you taking his bride and all. Okay, what all you having?"

"Two burgers with everything and home fries. Also, two ice teas, sweet," Griff said.

Casey scribbled down the order and set off. As soon as he rounded the corner out of sight, Tessa heard him chuckle again. Since the doctor seldom reacted outright to anything, she wondered what his doing so now meant.

It didn't matter; she had more important things to deal with right now. She pointed toward the kitchen. "You're eating every bite you ordered," she told Griff. "I'm not going to cancel the wedding because I burst out of my gown."

"No, you'll cancel it because you don't really want to marry Clay."

"Who said I don't?" She watched Griff's blue eyes narrow, but then she thought of something and looked back to the doorway through which the older man had disappeared. "You know, Doc Casey has e-mail, and he seemed uncommonly glad to see you."

"Whoever wanted me down here to stop the wedding would have had to know what my e-mail address was. I never gave it to Doc Casey."

"Well, who did you give it to?"

He shrugged. "My parents, Clay, Sadie—"

"Shoot, if you gave it to Gran, the whole town could have it." Suddenly Tessa sat up straight and frowned. "My grandmother never told me she was staying in touch with you."

"She didn't stay in touch with me, apart from an electronic Christmas card or two. I just wanted her to have my address in case she ever needed me." *Or if you did,* Griff added silently.

Relieved that her grandmother was not reporting her every move to Griffin Ledoux, Tessa found her thoughts wandering to the enticing way the muscles in his shoulders had moved when he'd shrugged seconds ago. And that made her think more unwanted thoughts, like how good it had felt to be held by him ten years ago, when her dreams centered around having the perfect family with Griff, someday, when they were both ready—but there was no sense thinking about that. It was too late, too much had happened.

Someone came through the front door, making the bells on it jingle. The arrival reminded her that, at any minute, she and Griff could be joined by Clay and a whole bunch of her friends, and her grandmother Sadie.

They would part without anything resolved between them, and there would still be someone out there, this mysterious e-mailer, who had already known, or guessed, too much about her life, and was maybe itching to tell Griff more.

"Okay," she said, "let's get this conversation wrapped up. I need to call Clay so he can bring me back to the wedding."

Griff leaned back in his chair and met her stare for stare. "Since you aren't in love with him, why exactly are you marrying Clay?"

"That's none of your business." Tessa's heart picked up its rhythm, and she took a deep breath to try to keep calm. "We aren't that close that I would tell you my secrets." They could never be that close again, she thought sadly. "I never cross-examined you about your marriage to Janie, did I?"

"My life's an open book," Griff said. Tessa couldn't believe he was as nonchalant as he sounded. "What do you want to know?"

"Nothing!" That was true. She didn't want to know the personal, intimate details of any facet of Griff's life, or risk an emotional involvement with him ever again. She'd learned her lesson the first time. Besides, it would ruin everything. She had to remain determined to do what was right.

"I caused my ex a great deal of heartache by marrying her for the wrong reasons, and that's why I'm trying so hard to get you to walk away today. I don't want the same thing to happen to you and my brother."

"You keep saying that. How do you know I would bring Clay heartache? You've been living elsewhere almost ten years, Griff. The Air Force Academy, then all that military service. None of us are the same people as when you left. Maybe marrying me would make your brother happy. Did you ever consider that?''

''Is that why you're marrying him? He's fallen in love with you, and you think one of you being in love is enough to hold you together? Because it isn't. I know this from experience. It won't give you your dream of a loving husband and a family forever after, Tessa.''

''I'm not discussing this with you.''

''Fine. Call Clay. He'll tell me what I want to know.''

No, Tessa thought, Clay wouldn't tell him. Clay, like she, would do anything to keep their secret, as would the only other person who knew—Sadie, her grandmother. Which made her wonder how this mysterious e-mailer could have possibly found out what he had, and what else whoever it was might know that he could tell Griff.

She couldn't chance Griff finding out anything else about her marriage to his brother. She had to get him to leave town.

But how? Sitting back in her chair, Tessa lifted her gaze to meet Griff's. If she pushed him too much to leave, would he begin to suspect there was something else behind her not wanting him there? Something that could change his life—and others'—forever?

Chapter Two

Before Tessa could decide what to tell Griff, the small cowbells on the front door jingled again and seconds later, two elderly men in overalls came into the section where she and Griff were, greeted the third man already there and sat down with him at a long table near the front of the room, all facing her. Tessa frowned. Doc Casey came in with her and Griff's ice teas, then stopped at the other table to take orders, wearing a totally unfamiliar grin on his face. As Doc Casey turned to head back into the kitchen, the bells clanged again, and another elderly patron moseyed in to join the other three.

"Just my luck," she muttered. "The bakery's mid-morning coffee club showing up in the afternoon to see the town's favorite deputy sheriff's intended bride meeting with his brother. By the time they're done building this story up, everyone's going to think I'll make Clay a terrible wife."

"They'd be right, but for the wrong reasons."

Her irritability level rose another notch, like mercury in a thermometer. She leaned in close to him and whispered, "You're wrong. Unlike you, who had to prove the only way you could be content is to be totally free, your brother liked being married." He'd loved his deceased wife Lindy tremendously. The whole town knew that. "Clay and I both want the same thing—to stay in Claiborne Landing among family and friends—which is why we will be compatible. That compatibility will bring us happiness."

Griff didn't say a word. He didn't have to. His eyes did his talking for him, and suddenly, Tessa realized how close the two of them were, almost face-to-face, mouth to mouth. She could feel his warm breath against her cheek. Without knowing how it happened, she found herself wanting, desperately, to kiss him.

Her emotions were doing her thinking again, that's how it had happened. She backed up abruptly. "Just how long are you going to be in town, anyway?"

"Long enough to figure out who made the effort to get me here."

"Why would that matter?"

"Somebody besides me thought you two getting married was not a great idea. I'm kind of thinking it might be good to stick around long enough to find out who and the why behind it. Stock up ammunition."

"It's a wedding, Griff, not a war."

"Divorce *is* a war, and I figure that's where you two will eventually wind up if you don't think this through all the way."

Tessa groaned. She was going to have to get Griff out of town, and the sooner, the better. To not do so could only lead to disaster.

"I'm going to call Clay." She rose and turned as

Doc Casey rounded the corner again, this time carrying catsup and mustard bottles to the other table. Then she remembered Sadie had her purse, and she would need a quarter for the pay phone. Rather than ask Griff for anything, she walked up to Doc Casey to ask him to let her use the phone in the back, just in time to catch his last words, "Don't worry, boys. Things'll pick up right soon now."

"Looks like you're having a sudden surge of business, Doc." She frowned with disapproval. "Could it be the entertainment?"

Doc Casey's eyes twinkled. "Naw. There hasn't really been any."

"That's good to hear."

"But there's fixin' to be," he added gleefully. "Clay just arrived."

"You called him?"

"Have to stir up the pot for the audience," he said, without one lick of guilt whatsoever coming from him.

Sure enough, the now grating jangle of the bells announced Clay's entrance through the front door. He saw Tessa and came to the doorway between the dining rooms, where he stopped and stared from her to his brother with a look that asked them both, *What now?*

Her heart went out to him. Clay had had enough to deal with being a deputy sheriff and a single father to a six-year-old for the past year after his wife Lindy's death from cancer; he didn't need to be in the middle of an argument between his only brother and his soon-to-be second wife, and definitely not in front of the biggest gossips in town.

"Doc, sometimes you go too far," Tessa said, indicating the elderly men with a nod of her head.

"C'mon, Miss Tessa, don't spit bullets over this.

Deputy sheriff's fiancée gets carried off from the wedding by his own brother and ends up here? Biggest thing to happen around Claiborne Landing in ages. Usually Athens sees all the action. If this had been happening at your grandma's doughnut shop, she would have called in her favorite customers, too. Have to be loco not to.'' Doc Casey lumbered over to the other table and left her to deal with Clay.

"Tessa, *what* is going on?'' he asked quietly, his face now unreadable.

"Your brother kidnapped her, deputy!'' the old man next to Tessa said. "Picked her up, plopped her over his shoulder and carried her right out of the church.'' He slapped his knee with his Casey's Kitchen cap. "Wish I'd a been there.''

Tessa glanced at Griff, who was frowning at both of them. She frowned right back. If he'd only been ten minutes later, she'd be married to Clay and wouldn't be in this predicament. Speaking of happiness, well, to say the least, she'd been happier. A lot happier.

Like when she'd been in Griff's arms. She hushed that thought away and turned her attention back to Clay, the one she couldn't let get away, the same second as Doc Casey reappeared with a tray, headed for Griff. With this anonymous e-mailer loose, she didn't want to let anyone alone with Griff for long, so she grabbed Clay's sleeve and led him well away from the table with the elderly customers, to an empty area where she could talk softly to him without being overheard and still keep her eyes on Griff. Even across the room she could feel his eyes on her. Warmth drifted up through her body like the smoke before a fire.

"We've got to get Griff out of here. Someone sent him an e-mail telling him we aren't in love.''

"So he came and kidnapped you from the wedding." Clay ran his splayed fingers through his wavy black hair, looking, Tessa thought, as disconcerted as he had after his wife's death over a year before, only without the pain this time. "Who would send him news like that?"

"I don't know," Tessa said grimly. Noting with relief that Casey didn't say a word to Griff as he delivered their food, she gestured for Clay to lean down. "What I'm worried about is," she whispered, "what if this person somehow has found out the truth behind our engagement, gets Griff aside while he's here and tells him. We can't let that happen."

Clay agreed. "I'll stick to him like glue for the rest of the day, but after that, since I'm not getting married today, I'll probably need to go back to work."

"After that," Tessa said, "it's my turn anyway. What we need is a way to make him leave. If he does, maybe the e-mailer will think Griff doesn't care about our getting married and leave him alone."

Clay gazed down at her for a long minute. "I think I might have an idea, but let me think about it. I'll let you know. You sure his leaving is what you want?"

"I swear," Tessa said. "Where Griff is concerned, I'm ice." She'd have to be. Everyone in town knew that she'd been in love with Griff Ledoux when she'd been younger, even while he was in the Academy. It hadn't been easy to convince them all that she'd fallen for Clay. But the people in the town were family, and she cared what they thought of her, so she had. She wasn't about to gamble with her future now by showing that she had any feelings at all left for Griff.

Even though she did. Just physical, she assured herself, but even that was more than she wanted to deal with.

"What about the wedding?" she asked.

"It's off for now. The pastor had another one in Ruston to get to. I told everyone we'd be in touch. I think they headed over to your grandma's for the free food."

"Let's hope that's where they went," Tessa said, staring grimly at the small crowd in the diner watching them. "We sure don't need any more help here."

Across the room, Griff worked on the burger Doc Casey had brought right before Tessa started whispering in Clay's ear, which had made Griff tense up inside something awful for some reason. His brother said a few words, then Tessa looked at Clay with those jewel-blue eyes of hers, and her hand briefly brushed Clay's sleeve. Griff felt a sudden flush of heat as though it were he whom she was touching. He quickly pushed down the surge of jealousy that followed, fully aware he had no right to that feeling.

The two of them began to walk over, and he quickly reminded himself that his intentions were very honorable. He was only there for one reason—to make sure they weren't fixing to do something they would regret, leading to a bad marriage. As soon as he was sure, then he'd be gone, since he had no right in Tessa's life. He knew full well he wasn't the settling kind. No use fooling himself about that. It was just too bad that seeing Tessa again had been an uncomfortable reminder of what he had missed out on.

"Kidnapping, Griff?" Clay asked, making no attempt to keep his voice down. "If this is a joke, it's not very funny."

Griff could say the same thing about his brother marrying Tessa, knowing how close Griff and she had been at one time, but he didn't. It wasn't the place. Besides, he was here to convince Clay to call off the wedding, not to end up in a brawling heap with his own brother.

Turned out he didn't have to say anything in reply. One of the old men from the other side of the room slapped his thigh and called out, "Not funny? It's pretty darn amusing to us, Deputy!"

"Better than the *Two Worlds Collide* soap opera," the grizzled man next to him, Jasper Tremaine, agreed, grinning. "Where's your sense of humor, Clay?"

"Must have left it behind at the altar," Clay said.

Jasper chortled. "Yeah, marriage has a way of turning a man grim, that it does. But that usually don't happen until *after* the nuptials and the honeymoon."

"Yeah, well, most people don't have a brother like Griff, either," Clay said amiably enough, but Griff could feel the tension behind his words.

The strain wasn't evident to the other side of the room, though—they were all laughing. Bemused, Clay shook his head as he sat down next to Griff, taking the seat Tessa had formerly vacated. "Now I remember why we didn't invite that bunch to the wedding."

Tessa shook her head as she slipped into a chair opposite them, her back to the elderly onlookers. "We didn't invite anyone but your parents and Sadie. *She* was the one with the stamps."

"I take it Tessa told you about my e-mailed invitation?" Griff asked Clay. When his brother nodded, Griff suggested, "Maybe Sadie sent it."

Tessa's gaze flew to him. "I don't think so. Anonymous isn't really my grandmother's style."

An uncomfortable silence fell over the table and, at

last, Clay asked the question Griff had been expecting. "So why did you steal Tessa away?"

"I haven't done that yet," Griff replied, his eyes penetratingly intense. "Have I, Tessa?"

"Of course not," she protested, bracing both hands on the table and taking a long breath. "And neither are you going to. Clay and I are still going to be married."

"So why aren't you two already driving back to the church?" Griff said, picking up his burger.

"The wedding has been temporarily postponed," Tessa told him. "The pastor had another engagement."

"Good." Griff barely kept himself from grinning.

Clay's already grim expression deepened even more. "Yeah, well, since you're so pleased about it, and it's all your fault anyway, we'll let you be the one to explain everything to Sadie. She's already madder than a wet hen. Make sure, little brother, that you take all the blame."

"Guilty," Griff agreed. "I'm surprised she isn't here with you."

Clay began to loosen his tie as he spoke. "I took off right after I told everyone the news to avoid Sadie's questioning me. I doubt she'll look for us here." He indicated the second plate that was in front of him. "You want that?" he asked Tessa.

She shook her head. "You can eat Griff's food after what he's done to our wedding?"

"The way I figure it, he owes me a meal after the worry he caused me. I thought you'd changed your mind, Tessa."

"Never!"

Her reply came so swiftly, Griff's eyebrows rose in question. She lifted her chin. "One broken engagement in a lifetime was enough."

And they all knew what that referred to. As she and Griff did battle with their eyes, Tessa was wondering if there wasn't something to what he'd said earlier about war. Oh, no, he'd meant with divorce. The two of them weren't even close, let alone married. It beat her why she would have purposely struck out at him with words, wanting to get a reaction out of him.

"Yeah, well…" Clay removed his tie and placed it on the table in a heap, as Griff continued to watch Tessa. "It's really too crowded to talk privately here, and the food's served. No sense wasting it."

"No sense," Tessa echoed, feeling stunned. Griff broke eye contact and ate another fry. Men! How could they be so peaceable about the whole thing? *Her* insides felt topsy-turvy, and her emotions were in an uproar with Griff so near.

Making a decision, Tessa rose. "Griff, I'm sure Clay can straighten you out a lot better than I ever could. He's had years more practice." She didn't have anything more she wanted to say to Griff, anyway. She'd said it all years before, when she'd broken it off with him. "I'm thinking that you'll reconsider and be leaving town just as soon as you have a chance to talk to Clay privately, so goodbye, and take care of yourself."

Griff rose swiftly and came around the table to take hold of her arm. Tessa didn't wish to be reminded of how warm his hands could be on her body, or how gently he could caress her skin, but she could feel his heat through the satin as his thumb stroked her forearm, and was powerless to break away, even with Clay and everyone else there, witnessing everything. They silently looked at each other, neither moving, until a voice sliced through whatever it was holding them together.

"You get your hand off my granddaughter, Griffin Ledoux. She's been spoken for." Like a bolt of lightning, seventy-year-old Sadie Newsom herself appeared in the space between the rooms, still decked out with the pink rose corsage, burgundy silk dress and matching hat she'd worn to the wedding.

Griff dropped his hands to his side. "Yes, ma'am." Almost immediately, Tessa felt her cheeks flush. Now she'd done it. The only thing she could think of to do was to play innocent.

"Grandma, I'm glad you're here. I need a ride home."

The cowbells started ringing steadily as Sadie was swiftly joined by two other ladies around Sadie's age, her closest friends, sisters Claudette and Reba, and by an assortment of ten or so other guests, all in their Sunday best, and all looking rather perturbed. Tessa couldn't blame them. She was feeling that way herself.

"Not so fast, Tessa." Peeling off one of her white gloves, Sadie marched right up to the three of them. "You put that tie right back on and get out of that chair, Clay."

"Yes, ma'am." Clay agreed and rose to his feet out of respect for Sadie, but made no move toward his tie. "Why?"

"Because we're all fixin' to return to that church and wait for Brother Jonas to finish over in Ruston. I got to him before he left, and he said he could be back at the church after five. Are you three ready to go?"

"Yes," Tessa said, hoping the problem of Griff would go away if she were married.

"No," Griff and Clay said simultaneously.

Tessa's mouth fell open. Griff would say no, but Clay? "Why not?" she asked him.

"Yes, why not?" Sadie repeated, her mouth pursing.

"My brother and I have something to discuss, and besides, quite a few of our guests have probably gone home." He gave Sadie a smile of genuine fondness. "Since I know you want the wedding to be a memory you'll cherish forever, let's reschedule so the church is filled."

"Is that what this wedding is going to be, Tessa?" she heard Griff ask, his voice low. "A wedding you'll cherish forever?"

To a man she didn't love. With Griff's eyes on her, never wavering, Tessa felt the room grow close.

Sadie was not fooled. "You want to postpone your wedding so you can *discuss* something with your brother?" Sadie gazed at them all, one by one, her eyes lingering on Griff and then coming back to Tessa. A lightbulb seemed to click on, and Sadie nodded. "I guess you're right, Clay. No sense in rushing these things."

"It's not what you're thinking, Grandma," Tessa hastened to say. Sadie turned to her.

"Then what is it? What on earth pulled you away from your own wedding which I waited your lifetime for?"

"She wasn't pulled, Sadie," one of the elderly men informed her gleefully from behind them. "She was carried! Kidnapped right out of the church! When Doc Casey called, he said Griff had slung her over his shoulder like a sack of meal."

Tessa groaned.

Sadie moaned.

The elderly ladies tittered.

Sadie's eyes focused on Griff, blinked, then focused again. "Good grief. Is that how your mother raised you? No, I know the answer to that. That is not how your mother raised you.''

''I'll say,'' Clay interjected.

The side of Griff's mouth turned downward, and Tessa realized she was in trouble. Sure enough, he had something to say.

''I guess your grandmother wasn't the one who e-mailed me to come and stop the nuptials, huh?''

In reflection, Tessa thought, maybe she should have told Griff to take her into the woods to talk and let him drive until he ran out of gas somewhere. They would both have been a lot better off.

''Stop the nuptials?'' Sadie asked, looking from Tessa back to Griff in bewilderment. ''Why on earth would I want to do that?'' She slapped him with her glove. ''Or anyone else, for that matter?''

Griff looked as if he was going to laugh, and that would have been the end of him as far as Sadie was concerned—she demanded respect from anyone under forty, and quite a few over, too. Even though Tessa was annoyed with Griff and wouldn't have minded seeing Sadie unleash her irritation on him with Griff powerless to stop her, Tessa took her grandmother's arm.

''I have no idea why anyone would want to stop my wedding, Grandma,'' Tessa told her. ''But you don't have to challenge Griff to a duel over it. I'll forgive him—someday—and Clay's going to talk to him. Let's go home, and we can talk about rescheduling this wedding for a later date.''

''Later? How much later?''

With all the eyes staring at them, Tessa did not want to pursue this subject. ''We can talk at home,'' she told her.

''Yes, let's. Clayton, Griffin, we'll get this ironed

out there, and everyone—'' she turned to the crowd, most of whom were now displaced wedding guests, and gave a regal sweep of her arm ''—I'll let you know the rescheduled date as soon as possible.''

''I'll bet you five dollars they never make it to the altar,'' Jasper said to the man next to him. Reba, his wife, walked over and shushed him.

Tessa loved the community and almost all the townspeople and, normally, would have been grinning ear to ear at the old men's antics, but all she could think about now was that Griff was following her every movement with his eyes, and how much she needed to get out of there before she began to like it.

Tessa was almost to the door when the bells rang again, and a six-year-old boy with a Huckleberry Finn smile entered and grinned up at her. ''Hey, Tessa, where's my Dad?''

Grinning back, Tessa felt the stress of the day wane a little. Being around Jeb Ledoux, Clay's son and the real reason she was marrying Clay, now that his wife, Lindy, her good friend, had passed on, always had that effect on her.

''Around the corner, Jeb.'' She pointed. ''Who brought you?''

''Grandma and Grandpa,'' he said, referring to Clay and Griff's parents. ''They're looking for a parking space.'' He didn't move. ''How come you didn't marry Dad?''

''That's the question of the hour.'' Sadie sniffed.

''Grandma,'' Tessa scolded gently, then turned back to the boy she so badly wanted to be a mother to. Jeb looked confused.

''There was a temporary problem.'' Well, at least part of that was very true. Griff was a problem, but

Tessa could only hope he was a temporary one. "Your dad and I will be having the wedding as soon as we figure out how to fix it."

"Okay." Jeb darted off around the corner to where Clay was still sitting. Tessa lingered and watched as the child stopped when he saw Griff.

"Uncle Griff! You're back! We going fishing?"

"Come along, Tessa." Sadie nudged her arm.

She didn't have to be asked twice. Outside, Tessa hurried to Griff's truck and got her veil and gloves. With a wave at Griff's parents at the other end of the parking lot, she came back to her grandmother's car just in time to see Sadie fish her keys out of her dress purse.

Tessa reached for them, and Sadie frowned and slapped at her hand, the way only the person who raised you could get away with. Sighing, Tessa let Sadie drive, but made sure the passenger side air bag was turned on and her seat belt snug. Seconds after the elderly woman started the engine, she started in on Tessa, just as expected.

"Darling girl, how on earth could you let yourself be thrown over someone's shoulder and carted away?"

"It wasn't like that, Grandma," she said, gripping the armrest as her grandmother turned onto the highway and gunned the engine. Actually, now that her irritation had worn off a bit, Tessa realized that it had been exciting—which was Griff's way. Romantic, even... With her eyes closed, she could see Griff's image clearly in her mind. He was smiling, and touching her shoulder, and pulling her into his arms, and then he was—

"He didn't kiss you, did he?"

Tessa's eyes flew open. "No, nothing like that. He

wouldn't." And she didn't want him to. She swore she didn't.

But her grandmother's astute question pulled her back to reality. She definitely shouldn't be fantasizing about Griff Ledoux. "It's been over between us for years."

"Hmm. Sounds like you're protesting too much. Why on earth did he tote you off?"

"It was a joke on his brother," she said softly, staring straight ahead. Her grandmother seemed to accept that and fell silent, giving Tessa all too much time to think on the ride home about Griff, and what he was really doing back in Claiborne Landing for more than a day's visit.

One thing she did know for sure. As soon as Griff figured out he wasn't going to stop her from marrying Clay—couldn't stop her—he would be returning to the Air Force. He'd told her while they'd dated in high school that ever since he was a small child, the only thing he'd ever wanted to do was to fly planes, and the second he'd learned he could earn a free education at the Air Force Academy in Colorado and they would train him to fly, he'd worked all during high school toward that goal. Four years in the Academy and six years mandatory commission. Ten years of his life promised away meant nothing to him.

And everything to her, since she'd had such different goals for her life.

"Don't let his return mess up your life, honey," Sadie said unexpectedly. Startled, Tessa gazed over at her. "Make sure you reschedule the wedding with Clay. He's a good man, and he can give you what you want."

A perfect family, and a home in what she thought

of—after a childhood on the road with parents who made dysfunctional sound fun—as paradise. Claiborne Landing. A place she never wanted to leave again—and where Griff usually never stayed long enough to hang up his hat.

"I know he can."

"And you've already got a lot between you. Don't mess up your chances like your mother did."

"You never talk about Mom," Tessa said, reaching for her gloves and holding them tightly in her hands.

"You look a lot like her." Sadie shot a smile in her direction as she turned onto the highway that would take Tessa and her to where they had split a two-story home into their own apartments. "But you're a lot more levelheaded. You didn't go following Griff around the world like she did your father. That's no kind of life for a married couple. Let alone kids."

"She did want to come back home toward the end," Tessa admitted. "But Dad always promised her there was more fun around the corner, if she would just stay with him. That he needed her, couldn't survive without her. So she kept staying, even though she hated the life we had. The bill collectors calling, the skipping out at night on the rent. She spent a lot of time crying." Just like Tessa had, when Griff had left and she'd known it had to be over between them.

Sadie sniffed. "Men always think there's something better around the next corner. What is it with them, anyway?"

It was a rhetorical question, one that both Sadie and she had asked themselves many times while she was getting over Griff.

"You never told me all that about your parents before," Sadie added.

"I didn't want you to feel badly, I guess." It had been worse than she'd ever admitted to Sadie. Her father had left her with her mother, who'd had pneumonia, Tessa had been told later, not wanting the responsibility of either of them, she supposed. She'd only been eleven, but she'd nursed her mother until she'd gotten really bad, and then Tessa had called the police for help, not wanting to, knowing that when they took her mother away, she would die and Tessa would never see her again. She'd been right. Her mother's heart had simply stopped beating. The doctor had said it was a defect in a valve, but Tessa had always figured her mother had died of a broken heart.

Afterward, she'd ended up without a real family in foster homes for almost a year, before she'd remembered where her grandmother, whom her mother had hardly ever talked about, lived. Sadie had come for her as soon as she was called, and Tessa had made every effort to put her former life out of her mind.

"I really thought I'd forgotten all of it, but the memories seem to pop up when I'm upset."

"Or when Griff comes to town, you mean."

"I suppose so." Tessa willed away the sad heart she always got when she thought about the distant past. "Anyway, he knows I want to be married and have children. As soon as he figures out the e-mailer was wrong and Clay and I will be perfectly happy together, he's going to leave."

"You think so, huh?" Sadie pulled into their driveway.

"Why wouldn't he?" Tessa asked.

"Maybe the boy has figured out what your father never did," Sadie said as she proceeded slowly up the two hundred slightly rutted feet to their home. "That the grass doesn't get any greener than right here in Claiborne Landing.''

"He can't stay here, Grandma,'' Tessa said, her stomach doing funny flip-flops at the very thought. "It would ruin everything.''

"Then you'll do what you'll have to to make sure he has no reason to stay, won't you? Hard as that might be.''

And it would be. As long as Tessa could remember, she'd dreamed of having a husband who doted on her and her children. When she'd met Griff, she'd thought he would be that man—right up to the point where his dream had become more important than hers and she'd broken it off with him, because she didn't want to ruin his life the way her father had ruined her mother's by his extreme need.

Sadie had been wonderful, of course, but Tessa had this dream of being part of the perfect family, and once she'd realized that the dream would never come true for her as a child, she'd changed to wanting to create it as a mother. With all her heart. If she married Clay, she would have Jeb—and, after all that had happened, that would be her dream come true.

The trouble was, while Griff was in another state, she could easily tell herself she didn't love him anymore until she was blue in the face. But now that he would be so close to her that she could reach out and touch him anytime she wanted, well, she was a little afraid that the electricity that still sparked in the air between them might become a higher voltage than she could handle.

She would just have to, that was all. Jeb needed her as his mother, and that was that. No one at all could be allowed to stop the wedding, not even Griff.

Not for any reason.

She wondered, worriedly, just how clear Clay was making all of this to his long lost brother, whom she definitely didn't love.

Or at least that's what she tried to tell herself.

Chapter Three

Jeb came running out of his bedroom to where Griff was sitting on Clay's couch, with tousled hair and a grin a mile wide, fully changed from ring bearer back to normal kid.

"Dad said I could stay with you or with Grandma, since he's going to work," Jeb told him. The three of them had come to Clay's house, a couple of miles from Casey's Kitchen, in the too quiet village of Athens. Too quiet at least from Griff's viewpoint. He never understood why Clay seemed to like it just fine—in his eyes, they'd locked up excitement a long time ago and thrown away the key.

"He did? So which one did you choose?"

"Here, with you. We can talk about going fishing tomorrow!"

"Yeah, just don't wear him out," Clay said, joining them after having changed into his deputy's uniform of a tan pullover and slacks. "He's going to be driving back to North Carolina soon."

"That was subtle," Griff said, with a friendly grin to keep Jeb from sensing the underlying tension that had been between them ever since Clay had entered Casey's Kitchen, whether Tessa had noticed it or not.

Clay didn't respond, but since Jeb was staring back and forth between them with a puzzled look on his face, Griff decided to lighten up.

"Thanks for letting me stay here," he added.

Clay shrugged. "Yeah, well, when I saw you and the folks together at Casey's, I figured it might be easier on all concerned if you didn't have to stay at the farm. You were kind of stiff with each other."

"I should have come home more often."

"Yeah, you shoulda," Jeb broke in, gazing up at him with something close to hero worship. "I missed you."

"I'm surprised you remember me at all." Griff ruffled the child's black hair and smiled back. "I brought you something." Lifting the suitcase by his feet onto the couch cushions, he unzipped it, took out a model of a C-130 Transport he'd bought at the base, and handed it to Jeb.

"Thanks, Uncle Griff!" If Jeb had sensed the tension in the room, the plane did the trick. He started making engine noises as he "flew" it around the living room. Clay left them for the kitchen and returned in seconds holding a beer and a soda. Standing in the doorway between the rooms, he regarded them both without any expression on his face, still angry, Griff figured, at what he'd pulled earlier.

"Look, Dad! I'm a pilot!"

Griff held back a smile, but a grimace flashed across Clay's face. "Better fly crop dusters in-state, then, son. If you travel all over the world like your uncle Griff, you'll break Tessa's heart. She's still going to become your stepmama, you know."

"I'll bring her with me!" Jeb said, filled with enthusiasm for his new career.

Griff and Clay shared a look. "Some women aren't movable, Jeb," Griff said, ignoring the jab to his heart Jeb's words had innocently caused. "Take it from me."

Clay finally moved forward and handed Griff the beer, and opened the cola for himself. "Why don't you go show your jet to the twins?" he suggested to Jeb.

"Okay." Jeb hurried over to Griff. "I'm just going across the street. Will you be here when I get back?"

"I'm going to stay with you while your dad works tonight, remember? So I'll be here at least overnight," Griff promised. Out of the corner of his gaze, he saw Clay's face darken. Good thing Jeb's attention was totally on him.

"Oh, yeah. When I get back, I'll show you all my favorite trucks, and my rock collection, and—" Jeb leaned close to whisper in Griff's ear "—the frog I have in my room that Dad doesn't know about."

"That's a plan," he said solemnly. Maybe he'd put the frog in Clay's bed tonight, remind his brother what fun was. Watching Jeb hurrying through the front door and letting the screen door bang shut behind him, Griff finally let himself grin again. The kid was irresistible. He did regret not coming more often to visit him, but visits with Clay, his wife and Jeb had always reminded him of what he could have had with Tessa— a family of his own by now, if she'd been the movable kind.

"What's with you, Griff?" Clay asked, a steely edge to his voice Griff hadn't ever heard before. "First you try to steal my bride, now my kid? He's taken to you like burrs to socks."

"Can Tessa be stolen that easily?" Griff remembered Clay's words in the restaurant about "stealing" Tessa away, right before he'd decided not to argue there. Looked like they were finally going to get into it. "If she can, maybe you two ought not to be getting married."

Clay gave him a dark look, then turned away to pace to the window and back again. "She's going to marry me as soon as you leave," he said, his voice gruff, "so you'd probably be better off just visiting for a bit, then going, and saving her—" Abruptly he stopped himself from saying more by taking a swig from his can.

"Saving her what?" Griff asked.

"Nothing. It's just," Clay continued, "that Tessa is over you. She wants to get on with her life. I'd hate to see her upset because you're back here. Any more upset than you've already made her, anyway."

"But you two shouldn't be getting married. You don't love each other—"

"Did I say that?" Clay interrupted, his face tightening just like it used to when they were kids before he would sock Griff in the gut over something. "Did she?"

"Neither of you will say you do," Griff pointed out, tensing up, "which makes me suspicious."

"Neither of us has to say it, because our getting married is none of your business, Griff."

"Someone must think it is, or they wouldn't have sent me the e-mail."

Clay finally sank down in the chair across from the sofa, having said a lot more than Griff remembered him ever saying at one time. He figured it must finally be his turn to talk.

"You two will make each other miserable if you aren't in love. Hell, Janie was in love with me, and I still made her miserable because I wasn't in love—"

"I told you," Clay said, rising, "I'm not discussing this with you."

"I'm only thinking of Tessa's best interests—"

"Too damned late for that, don't you think?"

"It won't be too late until you have a ring on her finger." Griff rose, too, glaring back.

"I told you, this is none of your damned—"

"You two stop that, and right now!"

Griff's eyes flew to the screen door, through which Tessa was entering, and, not wanting to have her see how much physical energy he was putting into fighting to keep her single, he willed himself to calm down. She had changed into jeans and a delicate pink T-shirt with those thin, spaghetti straps for sleeves, and brushed her hair out so that it fell in loose, crinkly waves over her shoulders. She was a slightly older version of the teenage Tessa he'd left behind, and Griff had never wanted her more.

He quickly shoved his desire back down, knowing full well that he still couldn't give her the happiness she wanted. But an aching emptiness remained in his chest, the same feeling he got every time he came back to Claiborne Landing and saw Tessa. Or maybe he lived with it, and kept himself so busy he never had time to think about it. He wasn't sure anymore.

She stood there, frowning at them both. "Tell me you aren't fighting with Jeb in the house."

"He's across the street with his friends," Clay said.

"Good." She put her hands on her hips, and Griff

forced himself to pay attention to what she was saying instead of how great she looked. "I came over to tell you two your mom and dad called me. Since we're not getting married, Clay, they're changing the wedding celebration they were going to have for us next Saturday to a community get-together in Griff's honor."

"I don't need a get-together," Griff said. He just wanted to get the marriage called off and get out of town.

"They're your *parents,*" Tessa said, her eyes turning into sapphire steel. He found himself shifting uncomfortably under her critical stare, and feeling mighty guilty.

"I told them I would come and see what your plans were about sticking around *this time*—" she paused to let her point sink in "—and then get back to them."

"He's leaving tomorrow," Clay said.

"You are?" Tessa's eyes widened in surprise.

Griff could have sworn he saw disappointment brush across her face. But before he could answer her, she nodded and said resolutely, "That's for the best."

Griff wasn't so sure. Tessa had hesitated, but Clay had practically pushed him out the door. He felt as if something was going on behind the scenes here, and that he wasn't even brushing the surface of it—just like the rest of the e-mail, the part he hadn't told Tessa about, had said. It had given the particulars, then ended with:

Clay and Tessa might be getting married…but what's between them isn't love.

So what the hell did that mean—"what's between them"? What could be between them? And what in the world would it have to do with him? Even if he couldn't stop them from getting married, which he still very much hoped to do to save them from unhappiness—and poor Jeb, come to think of it, from being stuck in the middle of it—Griff figured he had to stick around to find out what was drawing these two together. If he didn't, whatever it was they were hiding was going to haunt him. Especially if they ended up miserable, like he was.

Had been, he corrected swiftly.

He would ask them outright what the other part of the e-mail had meant, but Clay was glaring at him, and he figured any more probing might just land him in jail so he'd be out of their hair. He wouldn't put anything past his brother in this mood.

"So I'll tell your parents that Griff won't be able to make it." Tessa turned to go.

"Not so fast," Griff told her. She stopped where she was and faced them again, confusion on her delicate features. "I never said when I was leaving—Clay did. I was thinking about sticking around a while. I'll let Mom and Dad know soon."

As clearly as Griff had read sorrow on Tessa's face the day he'd left for the Academy, he saw a sadness in her eyes that came and went, as he had in her life on his scarce visits home. Something wasn't right with her. He glanced at his brother and saw that his intense gaze was on Tessa, too, his eyebrows slanted with only concern. So whatever was between them that was drawing them together, it wasn't love.

The e-mailer had been right.

He ought to say to hell with it, get in his truck and drive home. Leave them alone to their future. They were adults. Maybe they would just have to learn their lesson about marriage the same way he had. Still, he couldn't shake the feeling that whatever was wrong *was* his business.

And, so help him, he wanted to kiss her. Just once more. Find out the fantasy he remembered wasn't the reality and get her out of his system. Then maybe he could leave.

"I have to go."

Just as suddenly as she'd come, Tessa was gone. Clay caught the screen door before it banged a second time as he hurried after her, and Griff was left staring through the screen at them both.

He was probably stupid, but he was going to stay until he found out what was really going on here. Not, he told himself definitively, on account of Tessa. He might still be attracted to her, but there was no way the two of them could ever make it together. She'd shown no signs of wanting to leave with him, and he— well, he wasn't so sure he was cut out for love anymore.

Tessa had one wild thought, when she heard the screen door squeak open for a second time, that Griff had actually followed her out to her car. Once she reached it, she turned, slowly, her arms folding over her pounding heart, steeling herself against whatever he was going to say.

But it was Clay. Her arms falling down by her sides, her chest heaving—she told herself with relief—she relaxed her shoulders.

"You shouldn't have run away like that," he said, leaning close so he wouldn't be overheard. "Griff had a look like he knew something was up between us."

"Something is up between us," she reminded him softly. "But what are we going to do about Griff? He can't stay. If whoever e-mailed him *has* found out why we're getting married, he or she might get to him and tell him.''

"Remember I said I might have an idea to get him to leave? I had a chance to think it through.''

"And?''

"What does Griff hate more than anything else?''

It took only seconds for Tessa to think of the answer. "Being tied down here.''

"So what if we tried to do just that?''

"But he *is* staying.''

"Of his own free will. What if I gave him the impression he *had* to stay? Tied him down?''

"He'd hate it.'' That had been the reason he'd left to begin with, Tessa knew. He was looking ahead and saw nothing but a life filled with the same old work and life he'd always known, and it had held no appeal. He hadn't given any indication it did now. He'd run, just like he'd run when he was eighteen.

"I think it will work,'' she said, nodding slowly.

"Only one problem.''

Her gaze flew up to his.

"You'll have to tell him, and make him feel obligated. He just saw full well I want him to leave.''

She could see his point, but that could well give Griff the wrong impression. Make him think she was having doubts. Caught, Tessa stared up at the large, two-story house that had been her best friend Lindy's pride and joy, but now had a closed-up look. Clay never bothered to open the curtains even. It was no way for Jeb to live. She wanted to put some light back into the child's life, and to do that, she needed to get married to Clay. And to do that, she needed to get Griff gone.

This was a horrible situation. At one time, she wanted nothing more than for Griff to stay, and now she was going to go in there and set him up so he would leave.

But it was the right thing to do, and both she and Clay knew it. For Jeb's sake.

"Just tell me what you have in mind."

Griff was pacing the living room, catching glimpses of Tessa and his brother almost cheek to cheek through the screen door. Jealousy was eating at him, but he knew he had no right. He paced away, telling himself not to look. Then he paced back and looked anyway. The two of them were discussing something outside, their faces solemn. By the time Griff got back by the door, Clay was striding toward his truck and getting in.

Griff stopped pacing. He'd already agreed to watch Jeb that evening, so Clay's leaving didn't bother him. However, Tessa was striding toward the front door, her face filled with determination, and that gave him pause.

This, he thought, opening the screen door for her, should be interesting.

Once on the porch, she glanced inside, then shook her head as she indicated the swing. "Please sit. I have something to ask you."

"You can ask, but I'm not leaving."

"So you said. That's not what I wanted to ask you."

Her eyes, so pretty with their dark, long lashes, gazed at him for a few seconds as she waited for him to take a seat. He found himself remembering how dark blue her eyes got when the two of them had made love. He moved outside and sat down on the swing. She took the wicker chair next to it, angling herself toward him, lifting her feet up onto the cushioned seat and wrapping her arms around them, looking closed in.

It probably wouldn't, he thought, be a good time to try for that kiss.

"Your brother and I have a favor to ask you."

"I'm not giving you away if you get hitched. You should have taken me up on it when you had the chance."

"That's not funny." Tessa counted to four—he could hear her—and took a breath. "And that's *when* I get hitched." She frowned and rolled her eyes. *"Married."*

He shook his head. "I wouldn't call what you two are planning marriage." Before she could protest, he asked, "Where is my brother, anyway?"

"He went to work. He said you were going to look after Jeb until he gets home late tonight. He's over there." She lifted a red-tipped finger and pointed across the street.

"No problem," Griff told her.

Tessa wondered whether to debate his earlier statement about her marriage-to-be, then decided Griff would love the chance to argue about it again, and she didn't want to get him started. "Anyway, Clay said since he didn't get married today, he can't take the vacation days he'd planned to this week, or he won't have them when we do get married."

Days off work to be with Tessa after the wedding ceremony. That would be called a "honeymoon," something Griff did not want to think about his brother taking with the woman he'd once loved, even though he was over her.

He was.

"Okay, so what's the favor?" he asked irritably.

Tessa took a deep breath. "We'd had a bunch of things planned for his time off. Things we were going to do together."

"Together?" His mouth went dry.

"So he needs to find someone to step in and do everything he promised to. Things I couldn't do alone, without him."

Thoughts of what those things could be on their honeymoon week made Griff shift on the swing, suddenly uncomfortably aware that he was physically reacting to the very idea of being alone with Tessa in the days to come. "You're asking me to step in?"

"Who better?" she asked confidently.

"To spend time with you, that's what you're asking me to do?"

"Yes," Tessa said slowly, not sounding so confident this time. Then she swung her sandaled feet down to the porch floor and sat up, looking him directly in the eyes. "Innocent stuff, Griff."

"Oh." He told himself not to feel disappointed. "How innocent can it be if we spend time together without Clay?"

"Very innocent," she said firmly.

"I'll bet you that's not what everyone in town who sees us together will think. And don't tell me the gossip wouldn't bother you." He knew better. Tessa loved this town and everyone in it. And as far as he knew, the townspeople had taken the almost orphaned young girl into their hearts as well—the people here were that good. Their gossip would hurt.

With a tiny shrug of her tanned shoulders, she turned her gaze on the house across the street. "No one will gossip. We're going to make it known that the only reason we're together is so that you can make amends for ruining your brother's wedding by helping him not to renege on his promises.''

''Is that the only reason we're going to be together, Tessa?'' he asked quietly. ''You don't have any ulterior motives, do you?''

''Of course not!'' she said, but she blushed. ''Remember, you're the one who stopped the wedding and messed up Clay's and my lives.''

''I didn't notice you screaming or trying too hard to stop me when I was carrying you out of the church.''

''Of course I did!'' she denied. ''I hit you, remember? I wouldn't be surprised if you're all black and blue under your shirt.''

''You weren't hitting that hard. But on the other hand, maybe I should check.'' Standing, he started loosening his shirt from his pants.

''Don't you dare,'' she said, standing up and putting her fisted hands on her hips. ''I swear, Griff, don't you take off that shirt with me here, or I'll do something drastic.''

He grinned and let his hands drop to his sides. ''So you are concerned about gossip while you're alone with me.''

''I am only concerned,'' she said slowly, ''about the people who won't get the help they need because you came here and messed up our plans. Now, are you going to step into his place for the next few days, or not?''

With Tessa included, it was an offer, Griff thought, that he could not refuse. Not that he was fixing to get involved with her again, at least not the forever-after kind of involved. No, he would be out of there as soon as he figured out what was going on.

And something definitely was. There was no other

reason for Tessa to want to stick this close to him, unless maybe she still had feelings for him. He gazed into her cool eyes. Okay, maybe not. Maybe she was afraid to leave him alone. But why would she be?

The e-mailer, he thought, tucking in his shirt again. She didn't want him around whoever had e-mailed him, talking to him or her. That had to be the reason. But what was she afraid he would find out? It must have something to do with him, or she wouldn't be so worried.

But what? If he found out, maybe he would also then know why she and Clay were getting married, and be able to come up with a more convincing reason to keep them from this farce they were about to enter into. But to find out, he would have to get away from Tessa and Clay at some point, so he could be approachable by the mysterious e-mailer. This was going to be some juggling act, because if he were right in his speculations, neither of them were going to let him get away alone for one second.

"Well?" she asked.

"I do owe Clay—" He moved his jaw as though he were still thinking it through, reluctant to say yes. "I guess I can substitute for him. But then I'm out of here."

Griff knew that Tessa was good at hiding her emotions from a long time of having to when she was a child, to keep her mother from getting depressed. So he was quick enough to see her true reaction to his words—hurt—before a stoic look came over her features. He hated that; he'd hurt her enough already. He reached out to cup her cheek, but she drew back.

"Honey—"

"That's Tessa to you." She pointed at him in emphasis. "We might have to stick around each other for a few days, but as far as I'm concerned, we're just two people who have a past, but no present and no future. Got it?"

"I wouldn't have it any other way, Tessa."

"Neither would I," she replied.

"I guess that means goodbye kisses are out, huh?" he asked.

With a throwing of her hands palm up into the air, total exasperation filled her face. "I'll see you tomorrow morning at eight o'clock sharp for our first good deed." Turning, she hurried down the steps.

"Wait—you didn't tell me where we're going," he called out to her. "Or how to dress."

"Wear an apron."

"Just an apron?" Now that didn't sound promising—or very informative—so he couldn't help but tease her just a little. "No clothes? Won't I catch a draft?"

She slammed her car door in reply. Well, that probably meant he should wear clothes. Good thing, as he figured the air was going to be really frosty around Tessa tomorrow.

Maybe, he thought, he should get his own plans underway tonight.

At home, her bare feet up on her cushiony sofa, ready for bed in a thigh length T-shirt, Tessa remembered Griff's parting words and had to smile, even though the situation she was in was serious beyond belief. *Just an apron.* So typically Griff, even after all these years. She had missed the sexual banter between them, just a little. Clay was always so quiet, had been since his wife had passed on. She knew he missed

Lindy—shoot, she did, too—and that she herself would never be a substitute. Sometimes she didn't even know what to say to Clay, so the times they'd gotten together, she'd concentrated on Jeb, and Clay had mostly watched the two of them interacting.

For the first time, her confidence in her goal of marrying Clay floundered. Was she making a mistake? Was this marriage the best thing for Jeb, as she'd thought ever since Lindy had passed away? As he grew older, would he come to feel the distance between her and Clay, and worry? Or worse, would he think that was how marriage was supposed to be—two people who had trouble talking to each other?

Stop analyzing this, she told herself. It wasn't like she was the only one who thought this was a good idea. Lindy had wanted it, had made the request of Clay that he get married again as soon as possible so Jeb would always have a mother. Clay had agreed to it. Sadie had even thought it would be best for Jeb to have Tessa there. No one had said "boo" when it was announced. So why was she still worrying?

Because Griff had come back and *he* didn't think it was a good idea. That's all it had taken. Hadn't she learned after she'd broken her engagement to him to think about what was right, and not about what her emotions dictated?

She was twenty-seven. It was high time she did.

The phone rang, jerking her out of her thoughts. Sadie was usually winding down to sleep at this hour, so she doubted it would be her, and she didn't want to talk to anyone else.

But it was Clay on the answering machine, and that made her pick up the phone. Clay never called her.

"Sorry to bother you," he said, sounding exasperated and frustrated, all rolled into one, "but there's trouble."

"Is Jeb all right?" Tessa whispered, her heart thumping.

"Not that kind of trouble. The Griff kind. When I volunteered to work tonight, I figured he would just stay home with Jeb. But then I ran into them at the Wal-Mart up here in Homer buying a tent. He's taking Jeb for ice cream and to hear the band at Casey's Kitchen. Then—get this—they are going camping."

"That's not in our plan!" Friday nights during the summer, Casey stayed open late and had a small, local country and western band play so folks in the area, especially the older ones, could get together in the air conditioning and have fun. The place would be packed. "No telling who he'll see!"

"That's why you've got to get over there. And just in case this mystery person who wants to tell him our business follows him out to Dad's pond to talk to him, you'd better bring a sleeping bag. I don't get off until after midnight, and I'm going to be too tired to baby-sit Griff."

Pushing the phone down into its cradle, Tessa ran into her bedroom to dress, muttering things under her breath she hadn't even heard since she was a kid.

You should just tell him the truth, a warning voice inside her head whispered. But she couldn't. There was no telling what the ramifications could be. Dang Griff! And dang her own treacherous feelings that had kept her from running down that aisle when she'd still had a chance this morning.

Chapter Four

For the Friday night dancing, Doc Casey had men pile the restaurant tables in a storeroom in the back and put the chairs along the walls. That was where Tessa spotted Griff, seated in one and leaning back, grinning at Jeb, who was line dancing with the adults.

For a few seconds, Tessa watched Griff watching Jeb. Her heart clenched as she thought about what could have been, if only Griff hadn't been so stubborn. To stop her thoughts from bringing her to tears, she took a deep breath.

She had no desire to sit there and converse with Griff, but she had to keep an eye on whoever might try to, so there was just one solution she could think of at the moment, especially since she didn't want to pull Jeb away from his fun to make him leave—not yet anyway.

Walking up to Griff, she dropped her purse in his lap. "Keep an eye on this," she called above the music, and then did some two-stepping that took her over by Jeb. The line opened to make room for her, and she started the heel, toe, heel, twirl quarter-way around, clap movement the others were doing. When she got all the way around again, to the point she was facing Griff, she saw that Jasper from Sadie's coffee club had settled down in the chair next to him.

Could Jasper be the e-mailer? What were the odds? She continued dancing, since she doubted if anyone would yell over the music to tell something of the magnitude of her and Clay's secret, but the second the song finished she grabbed Jeb's hand and tugged him the few feet to Griff.

"So you two are out for a night on the town, eh?" Jasper asked.

"No. The two of them were—" she indicated Griff and Jeb with a nod of her head "—and Clay asked me to come and make sure Jeb got home before Griff kept him up all night. He doesn't trust his brother much," Tessa told him, totally aware that Griff's ink-blue eyes never left her.

"I can see why, after the stunt you pulled today, Griff." Jasper chuckled at the memory. "So you came home to stop the wedding, eh?"

Griff loosened his gaze from Tessa to look at Jasper. "I came home because of an e-mail—"

Panic, like a tornado, whirled through her. "Griff, I hate to interrupt your social hour, but Jeb is young, and he needs to get to bed."

"But, Uncle Griff, you said we could go camping!" Jeb's happy face crumpled. They would be fortunate, Tessa thought, to avoid a full-fledged tantrum, because he was probably exhausted after the long day. She certainly was.

"Okay, camping then. Just let's go. I'm ready for

bed.'' Even if that bed was a folded quilt with a sheet over her. She glanced down and saw Jeb's gleeful look.

"Bed sounds good to me, too,'' Griff said, grinning at her.

"Going off camping overnight, hmm? Together?'' Jasper cackled with glee, and Tessa groaned softly.

"Separate sleeping bags, Jasper,'' Griff clarified.

"Separate *tents*,'' she added stiffly. "That's if I stay. I'm not sure.''

"Uh-huh,'' Jasper said agreeably, rising to go join his friends again.

"Grandma will have a cow when the gossip train reaches her,'' Tessa said as Griff lifted Jeb up to carry him.

"You didn't have to mention bed.'' Not expecting her to reply, he moved to drop some money into the band's bucket, since they played for tips. Seconds later, the three of them were out the door in the parking lot and quiet—except for the crickets, anyway.

"I take it Clay called you?'' Griff asked.

"He wanted me to make sure you didn't spoil Jeb rotten.''

"And that I didn't get to talk to anyone?''

Her horrified gaze flew up to meet his. "Not now, Griff,'' she said, indicating Jeb, who was staring at them both with wide eyes.

She could see his dark eyes probing her in the light from the security lamps on either end of the lot, but he dropped the subject and began walking. Gravel crunched under their feet as they headed toward his truck.

"So you're really coming with us?'' Griff asked. "I don't mind at all. How about you, Jeb? Do you mind?''

"Naw. As long as we can get goin' soon.''

Tessa's breath caught at the look in Griff's eyes. He wanted her to come camping with him—at his dad's pond. The very place where she'd made love with Griff, so many years ago now, for the first and last time. The very place where everything in her life had started changing. She'd been fighting going, not wanting to relive the memories.

But she knew she had to. On the way over, she'd reminded herself, over and over, of her basic reason for needing to camp out with them—Jeb. He'd been vulnerable since the loss of his mother and from the looks of things, was drinking in the attention from Griff. She had to come between them a bit to keep Jeb from bonding with him, so the child didn't suffer another loss when Griff left.

And no matter what her heart was murmuring to her about Griff's nearness right now, he was going to leave. Leaving was in his blood. She shouldn't fool herself. She could get hurt if she let her defenses down.

"Yes, I'm coming." As if it was ever in doubt.

Griff gave her a genuine smile that spoke of caring, and for one precious second, she connected with him again, right down into her heart. Forcing herself to cut the tie, she looked away as he said, "Good. It'll be fun."

Fun? She doubted that.

Minutes after arriving in the camping area near the acre pond about a half mile away from the home he'd grown up in, Griff took out battery-operated lanterns from his truck and checked the ground for red ant piles. It was clear. Next, out came the new tent. A few minutes later, after some muttering under his breath, Griff had erected a zippered shelter. She was impressed. The night they'd been together, it had been on a blanket under the stars.

"That tent is big!" Jeb said. "Big enough for three."

"Three six-year-olds, maybe," Tessa said quickly, her whole body tensing up at the thought of sleeping in the same small tent with Griff close enough to touch her, even with Jeb between them.

Griff put his thumbs and forefingers out to make a square that he pretended to look through, first at the tent, then at Jeb, then at her. "Hmm. I dunno. Seems to me we *could* squeeze you in, Tessa."

"I'm sleeping in your truck bed."

Griff looked doubtful. "You're going to be real uncomfortable back there, what with the mosquitoes and the hard floor."

"Tessa can have the air mattress. We men have our sleeping bags," Jeb said with a yawn.

He was so sweet, Tessa couldn't help but smile, and then she saw that Jeb was grinning up at Griff, and her heart broke. She was supposed to make sure the two of them didn't get close, and here she was standing there, and Griff was winning Jeb's heart. That couldn't be. Griff would only break it when he left them.

"That's very nice of you," Tessa told Jeb. "And if you find you can't sleep because the ground's too rocky, you're welcome to join me in the back of the truck."

"I'm roughin' it with Uncle Griff," Jeb said confidently. "I'm growin' up. Uncle Griff said so."

That hadn't worked well at all. Tessa turned back to her car to get the quilt she'd brought to sleep on out while Griff worked on the mattress and put it in the back of his truck. It wasn't long before Jeb was tucked into the tent on her quilt and sleeping. That left Tessa and Griff sitting on the open tailgate of his truck.

"You know, I was serious when I said the three of us could squeeze into the tent," Griff said. "Wouldn't want you to get scared."

"I doubt if I'll get scared. But thanks for the offer." She shifted position, and her sleeve brushed his. She shivered, and he reached back for a light flannel blanket and wrapped it around her. It was the same one he'd had seven years ago, the time they'd been there. The last time they'd made love, before he'd gone on to live his life, and she hers.

Gazing out over the pond that was dimly lit with lantern light, she tried to understand why she was almost wishing for the old days to be back. They'd been wrapped up in pain, as she spent hours praying for Griff to want to stay home, and hours more trying to accept that their marriage would never work. They were just too different.

Yet, there was no denying that it felt wonderful to be sitting here next to Griff again. She just had to fight her desire to lean into him and pretend that they were still lovers, and it was seven years ago....

"This feels good, doesn't it?" Griff asked softly. She remembered too late how easily he'd always read her, and she gazed up at him. His dark blue eyes met hers, and he leaned forward, and she forgot that it wasn't seven years ago. His lips met hers, and the second they did, she felt the same feeling that she'd always felt around Griff, right down through her body—delightful, sensual desire. For a few long seconds, she forgot everything and just basked in the feeling of being close to a man she had once loved more than anyone else in the whole world as she kissed him back.

Loved, before he'd decided his way was the only way.

The thought brought her back to reality, and she jerked away from him, stiffening up and pulling the flannel around her as though it were a shield to keep him from getting to her heart. She stared at him.

"You shouldn't have done that."

"Why?" he asked quietly. "Because you liked it so much it's giving you second thoughts about what you're getting into? Because you're worried that the yearning you just felt is the way you're supposed to feel about the man you're marrying—plus a whole lot more?"

More that she and Griff did not have together, she thought, annoyed at his persistence. "How do you know I don't feel that way about Clay?"

"Because you didn't kiss him when he came into Casey's. Because the whole time you were with him, you hardly looked at him and barely touched him."

"So?"

"So you used to touch *me* all the time." He paused to let that sink in. "And you never said goodbye to him when you left the restaurant."

"It was an awkward situation."

"You always said goodbye to me." The corner of his mouth turned upward. "With a long kiss."

Like the one they'd just shared. She couldn't let him see how it had affected her. "Yes, and that didn't help us to stay together, did it?"

He looked away and braced his hands on either side of the truck, as though he hadn't like what she'd said, but couldn't deny it, either.

"Which just goes to show you sexual compatibility has nothing to do with marriage compatibility," she added. "Clay and I are very alike in our thinking when it comes to marriage, settling down, and stability for the family."

"Stability as in staying in one place," Griff said stiffly.

"Exactly."

"You really hated traveling all over the country when you were a kid, didn't you?"

She nodded. "And I hated having Mom get sick and Dad walking out and not having anyone who cared around to help her—and me." She'd turned twelve the day after her mother had died, in a temporary care facility, with no cake, no friends, no anything. Alone. Marrying Griff would have meant more loneliness. Being by herself when he was on missions for days at a time, and losing friends and having to make a new life for herself and their children every time he was reassigned. No. She couldn't do that. Ever.

"I want to make sure any children I have will be totally secure, with lots of relatives and friends who will be right there for them if they need them," she told him. "And Clay wants exactly what I want—family and stability. They're important to him, and to me. That's something you never understood."

"Sure I did."

"Then why have you practically ignored your parents, your brother and your nephew while you've been in the Air Force?" Tessa knew she was playing on dangerous ground, but she couldn't stop herself.

"You don't want to know."

"I have to know," she insisted. There was more at stake here than just herself—there was Jeb's happiness.

"Because I couldn't stand seeing you and not having you—my way." He gazed at her.

"Your way, as in having me traipse after you wherever you decided to go."

"If that's the way you want to look at it."

She shook her head. "That's the way it would be. No thanks."

"Don't worry, I wasn't offering it."

"Well, it's good, then, that's there's nothing between us at all, isn't it?"

"Exactly." Nothing between them. Sure, Griff thought.

"Then stop blaming me for your not keeping in contact with your family," she told him. "It's not fair." Hopping down off the back of the truck, she retrieved a lantern from the picnic table Griff's father kept by the pond for barbecues, and walked down to the water's edge where she set down the light, reached into her pocket and threw something across the water.

Griff remained where he was. Was there another reason he didn't want to see his folks more often? Was there something wrong with him, that he didn't want to stay in one place for the rest of his life? It would be something to think about. Later. Right now, he had other things he needed to discuss with Tessa.

Pushing himself down off the truck, he joined her at the pond's edge.

"So what is this thing that's between you and Clay?"

Her mouth dropped open. She slammed it shut. Griff would have grinned, but by her reaction, he figured whatever her secret was, it was pretty serious. He also was fairly sure he wasn't going to get it out of her voluntarily.

"What are you talking about?" she asked.

"That's what else it said in the e-mail. That the

something between you is not love.'' He gave her a minute to think about that, but she said nothing, just kicked at the grass beneath her feet.

''If you don't want to let me in on your secrets, at least tell me why Clay sent you traipsing after Jeb and me.''

Not seeing any way out of telling him, Tessa took a deep breath. ''Jeb's been pretty vulnerable since Lindy died. We're worried he'll get attached to you, start expecting things out of you, and then you'll leave like you always do, and he won't know how to cope. So I'm here to keep reminding Jeb that you're going away soon.''

''So he doesn't get too fond of me,'' Griff said.

She nodded. The disappointed, hurt look on his face in the lantern light was enough to break her heart. But then he shrugged, and the hurt left his face abruptly. ''That's the way it's got to be, I guess. Doesn't bother me any.''

He was lying. But the fact was, she *was* holding something back from him, too, so she didn't feel as if she could challenge him. Reaching into her pocket, she retrieved another couple of pennies and handed one to him. ''Remember our game?''

''Whoever gets the penny farthest gets his wish.''

''Her wish,'' she said, which was part of their old game. ''Promise?''

''Sure.'' Reaching back, he let his penny fly, the same time she did, and they both skimmed the water so far out into the dark neither of them could tell who won.

''You've been practicing,'' he said in admiration.

''Nope. I've just gotten stronger.''

''I guess you have. Life does that to a person.''

"Life…and kneading bread dough for Sadie's 'To Die For' bread," she said. Thinking of Sadie reminded her of her own mission she needed to do—get Griff to leave town. While it still seemed to be a good solution, after their kiss, it had taken on more urgency. Which meant she should get moving on it as soon as possible.

"Speaking of Sadie, you know that first good deed that we're going to do tomorrow?"

"Yeah?"

"It's helping me at the bakery so Grandma can have a day off."

About to throw another penny in, Griff let it drop into the grass near his feet. The only thing he might wish for he wasn't going to get anyway—Tessa wanting to go with him. "Clay was *not* going to work in a bakery on his honeymoon."

"Sure he was." She lifted her eyebrows at him. "You promised to fill in for him, Griff. You can't back out."

Griff guessed the bakery was as good a place as any to make him accessible to whoever had written him. But the very thought of all that boring work for the whole morning was not his idea of how to spend his vacation. Tessa and Clay's happiness notwithstanding, his first inclination was to pack his bag and start driving away before the town started roping him back in like a wayward calf, and he was once again facing a boring life on the prairie.

But leaving, he thought with a feeling of sudden awareness, was probably just what Clay hoped he would do. And Tessa was in on it. They both wanted him to run, just as he would have before, and the only reason could be that whatever they were hiding did have to do with him.

He gazed at Tessa, who had a smug smile on her delicate mouth, as though she knew what he was going to say. "Sure, let's make Sadie's day. Why not? You said eight, right?"

Tessa felt her smile fading. He wasn't supposed to be this willing. "Right."

"Just enough time to get home and take a shower after breakfast, if we get up early enough. Better call it a night." He picked up the lantern and headed back up the hill to the tent.

She scurried up after him.

"Sure you don't want to share the tent?" he asked without turning around. "It'll be kind of snug, but we've done snug before."

She blushed. "I'll manage in the back of the truck," she assured him.

"Okay, but my offer's still open. If you get scared, just come on in."

"I won't get scared."

"Remember, there could be bobcats out here, what with the woods and all."

"That worked the last time we went camping, but it won't work this time."

"Why not?"

"Because I don't even know you anymore, Griff. We're strangers, and I'm not getting in that tent with you."

Griff had to admit that was true. When they weren't strangers, she never hid anything from him, as she was doing now. But what was also true is that he wanted her just as desperately as he had before they'd broken up. Maybe even more, with a kind of desire that made him feel like a stupid fool, since he'd been down that road with her one time before, and she'd left him eating dust.

When Griff went into the tent, silently, Tessa felt a feeling come over her that was unsettlingly familiar. Loneliness, the loss of warmth. Since she had nothing to do but stand in the lantern light, staring up at the stars, she was able to finally recognize the feeling.

It was the same feeling she'd had when her mother had died and she'd been left alone, left with empty arms and no one to hug.

It was the one that had been there when Griff had gone back to school and she'd realized she couldn't ever marry and leave Claiborne Landing with him, and she'd been left with empty arms, and no one to hug.

It was the one that had been there when she'd gone through nine months of carrying Griff's child, only to give her baby up and be left with empty arms.

And no one to love.

At the time, she *had* thought about telling Griff she was pregnant, but she knew he would have come home and done the right thing, married her and maybe gone to work on his father's farm, the very future he'd tried to escape. His father was certainly hoping for that, since Clay, the elder of the two brothers, had already gone into law enforcement in Dallas. But Tessa had been all too well aware of Griff's views on starting marriage on the wrong foot, with no money in the bank, and with their dreams on hold. He'd felt as if it would lead to disaster, and being in that position would make him terribly unhappy. She had worried that he would grow to hate his life, the baby—and her.

So when she'd been three months along, with Sadie sworn to secrecy about her pregnancy, she'd told everyone she needed to get away after her breakup with

Griff, and gone to Dallas with an idea. Knowing Clay's wife Lindy, her good friend, desperately wanted children but couldn't have them, she'd approached Lindy and offered to let her and Clay adopt her baby. Although sympathetic to Tessa, Lindy had also been ecstatic about the idea and somehow convinced a skeptical Clay. They'd agreed to Tessa's provisos that they move back to Claiborne Landing after the adoption was finalized so that Tessa could be around her grandmother and be a close "family friend" to the baby, and that none of them would ever tell a soul it wasn't Clay and Lindy's baby, not even Clay and Griff's parents.

Tessa had stayed with them in Dallas for the rest of her pregnancy, and for the six months after the birth that Clay and Lindy had been required to remain in Texas until the adoption was finalized, telling everyone back home Tessa was helping with the baby. The only sticky point had come when Tessa needed the father's consent for the adoption, but that had been taken care of legally—if not morally—with a thirty-day notice in the largest newspaper in Colorado Springs, attempting to contact Griff, which Griff never responded to. She'd held back his address, for the same reasons she'd decided this baby had to be adopted. As wrapped up as Griff was in school, Tessa hadn't been surprised he wouldn't have had time to look through every page of a newspaper, but still, she'd breathed a sigh of relief when the notice had been officially withdrawn and the adoption had gone forward.

When they'd returned to Claiborne Landing, everyone had welcomed Jeb as Clay and Lindy's child, and Tessa had been merely a smiling onlooker. It had been hard—was still hard—knowing Jeb was hers, but having empty arms.

Yes, she was good friends with this feeling of emptiness. But soon she would be marrying Clay and getting her son back. And her arms wouldn't be empty again. A stab of guilt went through her that she wasn't telling Griff the truth, but she couldn't. Clay was the only father Jeb had ever known. Griff's heart was still elsewhere, not at home, and she had no reason to think he would stay for a son any sooner then he would have stayed for the woman he claimed to have loved. But he might try to take Jeb with him, and she couldn't stand that.

It was better he just never know. It was better all around if he continued to chase his happiness elsewhere.

Even if she always would have an empty spot in her heart where he was concerned.

A noise somewhere out in the trees, sounding like a large cat, startled her. But Griff hadn't come out of the tent—she was certain of that because her gaze had remained intently on the zippered front after he'd gone inside—so she knew he wasn't playing some sort of trick on her. It occurred to her that it might not be a cat at all, but a person, which made her wonder who might have been watching her and Griff talking from the copse of trees not so far away. She had to admit now she'd been so occupied with Griff she wouldn't have noticed if someone had been behind them in full sight, close enough to hear what they'd said.

Bringing the lantern, she marched directly toward the quarter mile or so of trees between her and the highway, and could hear the elderly voices before she saw the women they belonged to.

"Oh, dear, I told you to leave that darned cat in the car! Now we'll never know if she was fixin' to sleep in the tent or not."

"I wasn't, Grandma," Tessa called out.

"I couldn't leave the cat behind!" Miss Reba protested, warbling out the words. "The woods are crawling with critters. It was either bring Thor or my gun."

"No gun! The last time you went loose with your pistol, you about blew off Jasper's peck—"

"Grandma!" Tessa called sternly toward the woods.

"Don't know how I even got that close," Reba sniffed. "It's not like it was that big a target."

"I did not need to know that," Tessa said, close enough now that she could see Sadie and her friend, Reba, side by side, Reba holding a huge, furry yellow cat, and her grandmother holding…binoculars.

"You were spying on us!"

Reba had the grace to look embarrassed, but Sadie stuck her chin out defiantly. "How else could I find out if you ended up sharing the tent with Griffin?"

"I'm not out here for that, Grandma." Tessa suddenly felt very, very tired. Exhausted even. The only thing keeping her going was that Sadie couldn't have seen her kiss Griff, or she would have said something immediately. "I'm just helping to keep an eye on Jeb."

"How was I to know that? You looked at that tent for so long I thought for sure you were about to go crawling into it. I knew it. I just knew this thing with you and Clay was odd."

"Grandma, I don't have to defend myself. I'm twenty-seven years old."

"That's a baby in adult years," Sadie said.

Only one sure fire way existed to stop this conversation dead in its tracks, Tessa thought. Changing the subject. "As long as you're out here," she said, "I need to tell you something."

The cat in Reba's arms lurched again and gave another long screech, reminding Tessa that she and Sadie weren't alone, and she would probably be better off choosing her words carefully.

Her grandmother waited expectantly.

"Griff and I will be working at the bakery tomorrow so you can have the day off."

"I don't need a day off," Sadie told her. "I like baking."

"Trust me, Grandma, you need a day off."

In the lantern light, Sadie's face looked even older than her seventy years and very wise. "I see."

"See what?" Reba asked.

"I'll explain later," Sadie told her, then turned back to Tessa. "This is going to backfire in your face, sugar."

"I won't let it," Tessa said, but in her heart, she was more than a little worried that her grandmother was right.

Chapter Five

Griff stood by Tessa, who was bent over a long work-table in the middle of the kitchen of the Shady Shoppe, expertly folding squares of pastry dough that were half stuffed with peach goo. Not goo. *Filling*—that was what she'd said. Oh hell. Even if he'd wanted to learn about making little pies—which he didn't—concentrating on what she was showing him was impossible. He was too busy watching the way her fingers danced over the pastries as she pressed the dough into place and made fancy scallops along the edge, and thinking about how her fingers had danced the same way over him when they'd made love—

"Ready to try making a pie?" Tessa asked, lifting hopeful, jewel-blue eyes to gaze at him.

He shook his head.

Tessa pursed her lips in disappointment as she bent over and started working on the second row of pies. Finally her fingers paused as she flexed her hands and gazed up at him. He was so quiet, and she had to know what he was thinking—if all this reminding him of what he had run from was making him want to run again. "I guess you find this all kind of boring, huh?"

"'Kind of' doesn't half cover it," he said, giving her a wicked grin.

"Smart aleck." She dipped her fingers in flour and flicked them, sending a white cloud of powder over his shirt, which he had refused to cover with an apron. "It might not be so bad if you got into the spirit of it."

"Okay, I'll get into the spirit of it." He dipped both hands into the flour, and she stepped back, her eyes narrowing. But instead of showering her with flour, he dusted his hands, grinned and stepped over to her mixing bowl where she had cookie dough. Taking out a couple of tablespoons full, he quickly rolled the dough into one miniature ball, then another, which he put on top of the first, and then a last on top of that. Some confectioner's sugar, two chocolate chips for eyes, a few red sprinkles artfully applied for a mouth, and he turned to her with a triumphant grin.

"A snowman."

She couldn't stop the smile that covered her lips.

He tried to transfer it to the baking sheet, but the head went askew, giving it a cocky look.

"A snowman with an attitude," he added.

For precious seconds, she laughed, and so did he. She'd forgotten how much fun being around Griff could be. She'd forgotten that the same spontaneity and love of life that had taken him away from her had been exactly what had attracted her to him in the first place.

She'd forgotten how wonderful it had been to kiss him.

Realizing this, she took a deep breath. "I need to finish the pies. Go wash the tables off, would you?"

She'd refused to let him up front where the customers sat the whole hour and a half they'd been working
there, so Griff figured he must have just flustered her.
For the life of him he didn't know how, but that was
all right since he wanted to be where he could be approached by the e-mailer.

Taking the spray cleanser bottle and a roll of paper
towels, he headed out into the small dining area. There
was only one customer, and she smiled at him and went
back to sipping her coffee from the white mugs the
shop used, which were heavy enough to be classified
as lethal weapons. They were the same mugs he remembered seeing on tables when he'd come here on
Sunday mornings with his mom to pick up doughnuts.
He had changed, Tessa had changed, but this area was
never going to change. He'd known it even when he
was ten, and that knowledge had felt like it was chok-
ing him around the neck for some reason.

Funny, it wasn't bothering him now. In fact, the familiarity was nice.

Whistling, he starting wiping down the tables, bringing himself closer to the customer to see if she might
be the one to approach him, but she ignored him. After
she left, he headed over to her table to collect her
dishes and found a dollar under the small plate.

"Didn't she pay you already?" he asked Tessa,
holding up the dollar.

Tessa took a quick look through the kitchen door
and then went right back to working on her pies.
"That's the tip."

"Pretty generous for less than a three dollar order."

"People love Sadie." *That should be obvious,* her
tone said. "And they know they get a lot for their
money here."

Griff brought the dishes around back. "That's why those pies are mostly peaches and very little goo."

"Syrup," she corrected without looking at him. "Sadie doesn't worry about profit. She's got the most generous heart in the world. I'll never leave her."

"You mean like I left my family? It isn't wrong to want to break away, Tessa."

"No, it isn't, anymore than it's wrong to want to stay with people you love. But somewhere along the way, you started looking at your family as something to be left, instead of something to be loved. And that was the wrong part."

He guessed she was right. But he had no idea how to fix the gulf between his parents and brother and himself, even though it would be nice. They had been apart for too long, he still had his dreams, and they'd all become nothing more than polite strangers.

The door opened, pulling him from his thoughts and causing Tessa to glance up and over the dividing section. "Oh, glory. Sadie's coffee club is here." The same crowd of retirees who had shown up at Casey's Kitchen the previous afternoon filed in, one by one, until six men seemed to fill the small front room.

"You think they're back to spy on us?" he teased.

She shook her head, her fingers flying over the little pies. "They always come in to have midmorning coffee. They're just a trifle early today."

"I'll handle them." Grinning at his opportunity to thwart Tessa's plans to keep him from talking to anyone, he launched himself through the open door.

"Griff—"

He glanced over his shoulder.

"Sure you can handle taking orders, Lieutenant?" The corners of her small mouth rose ever so slightly.

"After all my practice at work, piece of cake," he replied. She giggled. He stood where he was, watching her, enjoying the way her face lit up.

"You fixin' to take root there, *Lieutenant,* or get us some coffee?" Jasper called.

The last thing Griff wanted to do was take root anywhere. He grabbed the full coffeepot from the main counter and began filling mugs. When he was done, he put the pot back, grabbed the order pad and pencil from where Tessa had left them on the counter and stood next to the table, waiting for their orders.

"What happened to the cream and sugar?" one of the men asked.

Cream and sugar. Of course. Griff glanced up the countertop and spotted a large divided dish that held little packets of sugar and creamers. He put that in the middle of the table and stepped back, once again holding up his order pad. The men stared back at him.

"Spoons?" one finally asked.

Dang. This job wasn't as easy as Tessa made it look. Trudging back into the kitchen, he grabbed a handful of silverware out of a drawer, which, seconds later, he piled on the table.

"Help yourself." He got the order pad back out and stared around at the circle of open mouths, recognizing most of the faces as men he'd known forever. All except one. "Look, you all know this isn't my regular job."

"Good thing," Jasper interjected. The others snickered.

"I'm just helping out here so Sadie can have a day off."

"Where is she today?" the only stranger to Griff, a distinguished-looking man seated next to Jasper, asked.

Griff thought he seemed a little out of place among the dungareed men in his slacks and pullover sports shirt.

"I think she was heading to the boats in Bossier." "The boats" was verbal shorthand for the riverboat casinos on the Red River. "She'll be back tomorrow."

"So you're helping her out by trying to close her down?" Jasper asked, getting another round of laughter from the men, all except the one who had asked about Sadie.

"As if y'all would stop coming and risk breaking Sadie's heart," Tessa said from behind Griff. He turned, and she reached out and gently plucked the order pad and pencil from his fingers. "I'll take the orders if you'll go in the back. *Please* go in the back."

"But you need help."

"I know," she said with an exaggerated sigh. "Maybe I should call Sadie home."

He saw her eyes were twinkling, and she was barely holding back a grin.

"I guess I'm fired, huh? *Please* fire me," he said, mimicking her tone.

"No..." she said, and then her eyes got big as he grinned from ear to ear and started toward the door. "Griff, where are you going?"

"To pick up Jeb and go fishing," he said.

"You are not!" Throwing down the pad and pencil on the nearest table, she raced after him, catching the door just as he went through it. Outside, she caught his arm, laughing.

"Please come back, Griff. I promise, I'll let you be mean to the customers."

"You think that was funny, huh?"

"You did us a favor. After the likes of you, they've

learned what good service is. I'll bet even Jasper starts tipping.''

He laughed. She bit back her own laughter and stared up at him, trying to be serious. ''You can't leave. I want to go fishing with you, and I can't close until one.''

''It's safe to leave me alone with Jeb, Tessa,'' he said. ''I won't make any promises to him about staying. I'll even try not to get too fond of him.''

The air around them became deadly serious. Tessa swallowed over a lump in her throat and let go of his arm. This was all wrong, not the way it should be. Jeb should be Griff's number one fan.

''Oh, Griff, I am so sorry,'' she whispered, not realizing what she had said until the words were out and Griff's stare had deepened into puzzlement.

''About what?''

For a few seconds, she hesitated. She couldn't tell him the truth, so she searched her mind desperately for something else she could be sorry about. As she did, she realized there was a *lot* where Griff was concerned.

''I'm sorry things turned out this way for you and your family. I hope you can get close to them again.''

''Doesn't seem likely. Just like with you, there's too much water gone under that bridge.''

''I'm sorry about that, too,'' she admitted, stepping back, her heart clenching with sympathy. She couldn't fix what had happened between her and him—there would be no point in it anyway. They were too different still, and there was her secret that had to be kept from Griff at all cost. But she knew then, that in some way, in addition to keeping him away from whoever might have brought him here to begin with, she *had* to help him to leave town with family ties that were at least repaired, if not close. She didn't know how yet—she would need to talk to Clay about it. Perhaps he knew a way. "Very sorry," she said again.

"Yeah, so am I. People always say you can't go home again, and I guess that's true." He shrugged as though he didn't care, but Tessa knew the expression on his face, and the longing in his eyes.

He did care. He cared a lot.

The whole afternoon he was fishing with Jeb and Tessa, Griff tried to figure out what was on Tessa's mind. At one point, he thought he'd caught her gazing intently at him and Jeb when he'd leaned down to help the child with his hook, but then she'd walked over and picked up her purse as if she'd really been looking for that. Another time she had walked up to them as they were talking about Jeb's school, and sat down in the middle, as though she were trying to keep them separate, which was silly, since she'd already heard him tell Jeb he was leaving, probably after his parents' get-together picnic on Saturday. The truth be told, she was starting to get under his skin, coming in between him and his nephew, and he didn't irritate easily. Before he could say something he would regret, he decided it was time for them to go fill up his gas tank at the station on Highway 9 and then head home.

The three of them piled into his truck, since Tessa had left her car at home, where she'd gone after work to change into the tight blue-jean shorts and halter top she was wearing. As if watching her walk around in that outfit wasn't bad enough, Jeb insisted he sit by the window, which put Tessa in the middle—again—next to Griff, with her long, already tanned legs right there within reach. He swallowed and thanked God he didn't have a stick shift and a smaller truck. Otherwise he would have touched her every time he switched gears.

After he got gasoline, she was amazingly silent as Jeb chattered on, pointing out the new Athens post office, the church where he'd attended Vacation Bible School, and that the road crew had fixed the steep drop-off on the other side of the railroad tracks since the last time he'd been home.

"Good thing," Griff said as an eighteen-wheeler hauling a double-wide trailer coming in the other direction practically filled the two-lane road, and he had to drive on the grassy part to clear it.

Jeb watched the huge rig, his eyes wide, and said, "I'm going to drive trucks when I grow up!"

"You can't," Tessa said. Griff felt her shoulder touch his as she took a deep breath. He also glanced over and saw Jeb had leaned a bit forward and was frowning at them both.

"Why not?" he asked.

"I'd miss you too much," she told him. "Besides, you said you were going to stay right here and be a fireman not two weeks ago, remember?"

"Oh, yeah," Jeb said, and then fell quiet.

Griff was torn. On one hand, he could understand why, once Tessa was married to Clay, she would be reluctant to let go of her new little family because of her past. He could even sympathize. On the other, it seemed as though Jeb was starting to see the wonders of the world and what he could become, a pilot or a truck driver, and all he was hearing was "Tessa wouldn't like it."

He knew what that was like. No one had ever respected his dream, either, when he was young. His parents had told him they doubted they could afford to help him with college, and that they hoped both he and Clay would stay home after high school and help with the farm they would inherit. As he'd grown older and Clay had married and moved out on his own, finally becoming a police officer in Dallas for a while, they'd started laying on the guilt for him to give up his dream and stick around. Just like Clay, the day before, and Tessa, now, were laying on Jeb's shoulders.

"You can be a truck driver or a pilot, like you mentioned yesterday, Jeb," Griff said. Immediately Tessa turned to stare up at him, looking as if he'd betrayed her. He gazed back to the road and signaled for the turn down the long lane that led to the house Tessa shared with Sadie, and tried to fix things a bit. "Or you can be a cop, like your dad, or a farmer, like your grandad."

Tessa let out a faint sound of protest. So much for making her happy, Griff thought.

Jeb's face lit up with a big grin. Griff was glad Jeb couldn't see Tessa's scowl. He continued, "The only thing to remember is whatever you decide you want to do with your life—do it with your whole heart. You promise that?"

"Sure!" Jeb said, leaning back against his seat.

Parking by the house, Griff saw a car that hadn't been there earlier, along with a small pickup truck. "I think Sadie's back."

"Good," Tessa said. "Jeb, you can scoot inside and ask Miss Sadie for a drink, okay? I want to talk to Griff."

With typical six-year-old energy, Jeb opened the truck door and skedaddled around front to the porch. Tessa climbed out next, shutting the door and rounding the truck to open Griff's.

"Boy, that look hasn't changed in the last seven or so years," he said. He couldn't remember when she'd last cared enough about him to be this angry.

"Out."

"Couldn't we fight in here where it's cooler?" he asked.

Her head tilted sideways. "Surely the heat isn't going to bother you when you've been out in it all afternoon."

"That was just a little sunshine. You look like you're fixing to roast me in your grandma's double-decker barbecue pit with the gas turned up high."

"If you get too worried about a little heat, Griff, you could leave town. You're really good at that."

He got out. With a gentle push on his door, he walked over to Sadie's cushioned, green-and-white striped swing, sat down under the awning and stared at Tessa as she started to walk up to him.

"You've been ready to bite all afternoon, Tessa. Go ahead."

That stopped her cold. "I have not."

"Uncharacteristic quietness, long stares—I figure I must have done something wrong this morning. Go ahead. Tell me what it was."

Tessa gazed at the woods that bordered the yard. She had been watching him, but anger hadn't anything to do with why. Oh gosh. When she'd seen him with Jeb, the way they'd interacted, she'd started thinking about what could never be. The three of them together. He, Jeb's dad, and she, Jeb's mom—and Griff's wife—living with their son.

But she had been thinking about the impossible. Jeb belonged to Clay, and Griff belonged to his dreams. She had accepted both facts long ago, and the best she could ever do would be to marry Clay and fill a part of the aching gap inside of her. She was sad about that, but not angry.

"The only problem I have with you," she said, shifting her eyes back to him, "is that you would think of encouraging Jeb to think about careers that would take him away from his home. That's not right."

"Is it right that you want to stifle his dreams?"

"I am not. I'm guiding him so he makes the right choices. He's better off staying here with his family, not chasing after some dream that might never make him happy."

"Like your father?" Griff suggested gently.

"Yeah, like my father." Tessa sank down on the hard bench next to the swing and gazed down at the sand mixed in with the dirt at her feet. "And like you," she added, because he wasn't getting the point.

"You don't think I'm happy?"

"Are you?" she asked, really wanting to know. She wanted him to be. If he were happy, she wouldn't feel so badly—

"No." He shook his head. "And I'm not going to be, as long as I think you're giving up the possibility of falling in love someday to marry Clay. Don't you want more than that for yourself?"

"Once, I did. But I gave up on love when I let you go follow your dream." She didn't wait for him to comment on that. "How about you, Griff? Do you ever think you'll want love and a family?"

He rose and walked past her to look at the pink and yellow blossoms lining the side of the house a few feet away. Keeping his distance, Tessa thought.

"Sure," he said finally.

His admission startled her. He wanted love and a

family. Maybe he had finally come to his senses. The very idea choked her up, made her wonder if she should reconsider—

"But I don't think I'd be happy giving up what I've worked so hard for," he added, and the hope in Tessa's heart died as suddenly as it had been born, just as it had on the day she'd first seen their baby and accepted that she couldn't raise him herself—that she would have to give Jeb up so he could have a real family, something she and Griff could never be.

"Just what is it you have that you don't want to give up, Griff?" she asked, swallowing back her disappointment.

"Security. Freedom. Respect." He left the flowers and walked back over to her. "I've come to doubt if I can make any woman happy without compromising one of those somehow."

Needing to show him she had never thought otherwise, she gave him a tight smile. "It's a good thing I long ago gave up the silly notion that the two of us would ever be good together, then, isn't it?"

He nodded grimly. And as his gaze met hers, she knew that if she were to get any peace and happiness out of her marriage to Clay and being a mother to Jeb, she'd better make her pretense a reality.

"So what it all boils down to is that chasing your dream of freedom kept you from getting love and a family. Do you really want that for Jeb?" she asked.

He didn't answer. She would never know if he'd planned to, for a half a minute later, Sadie rounded the side of the house.

"You two come on inside. What on earth are you doing out in this heat?"

"Getting a few things straightened out," Tessa told

her, getting up to obey her grandmother. Sadie remained quiet as the two of them entered her downstairs apartment, going into the sunroom, as Sadie called it, where they found Jeb and the distinguished-looking man who had been at the bakery that morning seated at the table, snacking. The man must be relatively new to the area because Tessa couldn't remember having seen him around that much in the bakery. She was sure she'd been introduced, but new names hadn't been sticking at all lately, what with the wedding. Apparently, though, he knew Sadie.

And Sadie knew him.

"This is Horace Fortune," Sadie said.

Tessa frowned. Her focus changed from worrying about the tall, dark and frustrating man next to her, to the tall, gray-haired and mysterious stranger who rose and acknowledged her with a bob of his head. "I believe we met at the bakery."

"Did you drop by to leave a pastry order, Mr. Fortune?" Tessa asked, and then was annoyed to feel the jab of an elbow in her side. "What?" she asked, turning toward Griff.

Sadie giggled. *Giggled.* Her grandmother never giggled. "Horace came by because he's a friend of mine," she said.

"But all your friends are women," Tessa reminded her.

"Outside." Griff put a hand on each shoulder and tried to pull her back toward the door. She stood her ground.

"I could carry you," Griff suggested. Sadie giggled again.

Her jaw tightening, Tessa headed for the door, stomped down the stairs and walked toward the woods away from the house. Griff followed and caught up to her as she headed down a pine and oak shaded path, where she stopped and faced him when she thought they might be far enough away that no one would over-hear.

"First," she said, poking him in the chest, "don't you ever threaten to tote me off anywhere again."

"I thought you needed to get out of there before your grandmother got upset. I'm sure whatever is going on between her and Mr. Fortune is harmless."

"We don't know that," she said. "He's a stranger around here. And strangers aren't always harmless. Look at the havoc you've caused."

Griff regarded her for a minute, and she gazed down at the ground. Why was he bringing out the worst in her?

"I think your grandmother has had enough experi-ence reading people not to get bamboozled by a fancy dresser," he said, apparently choosing to ignore her remark.

Tessa wanted to smile, but she couldn't. "This is not amusing. I *care* about Sadie. I want her to be happy. I don't want anyone to dance in and out of her life, stomping on her heart in the process."

She said that, Griff thought, as though he were the one she was really referring to. He hated that he was going to leave Saturday with her thinking the worst of him. His pride wanted her to think the best of him, even if she no longer loved him.

And he thought he knew just the way. But first, he would need to talk to Jasper and find out what he knew about this man Sadie was giggling over.

* * *

Tessa's thoughts about helping Griff reconcile with his family simply would not leave her, so, early that evening, Tessa caught up to Clay at work, which was a block off Courthouse Square in Homer, a bustling town north of Claiborne Landing. He was heading out, so she walked back with him to his patrol car, keeping her voice low as she told him what she still wanted to do for Griff, despite the way he'd frustrated her that afternoon—try to help him reconcile with his parents.

Through it all, Clay kept quiet. Really quiet. She hated that about Clay—unlike Griff, she never had any idea of what was behind his dark-eyed stare. Griff always ended up telling her what was on his mind, either straight out or eventually, even if she didn't want to know. She found that comforting.

"So I was thinking that one of the other things we could have 'planned' to do this week could be to spend some time with your parents. But I don't know how to approach that with Griff. Since we just talked about that today in the bakery, I don't think he'd believe it coming from me."

Arms folded across his chest, Clay leaned against the driver's side window, and she stood in the empty parking place alongside, facing him. Around them cars drove by, people came and went, and she waited.

"I think trying to fix Griff's life is probably something you don't want to be doing if you want him to leave again," he said finally.

"Oh, I'm not worried about him leaving." Her heart tightened at the thought, but she ignored it. She wanted Griff to go. Absolutely. She was so close to being a mother again that she couldn't let anything go wrong. "I'm sure he'll go."

"Yeah?"

"You don't think so?"

"I figured nothing would bring him back to begin with." His eyes scanned the area around him, which she noticed he did a lot. Always on guard, always ready for…something, that was Clay. "I was wrong, wasn't I?"

"I guess."

"To tell the truth, I think he's really back looking for something he's been missing."

"Like maybe being home?"

"Like maybe you."

She shook her head vehemently. "He says he's given up on finding love. And I'm not in love with him."

"You don't want you three back together?" Clay asked, his voice tightening, his dark, troubled eyes finally gazing down at her. "As a family—you, Jeb and Griff?"

"No." She shook her head, surprised that he was actually talking to her about being Jeb's birth mother. They had always skirted the subject, and he'd never asked her what her reasons were for not calling Griff home when she was pregnant.

"I never thought it was a good idea, keeping Jeb secret from Griff," Clay said.

"You never mentioned why you agreed to it."

"Lindy begged and pleaded. She wanted a baby more than anything in the world. And me, I would have done anything for her," Clay admitted, pulling his sunglasses down over his eyes. "I'm not giving my son up, Tess, even if you do tell Griff."

"When I gave him to you and Lindy, I meant it," she said. "Jeb is yours. I won't tell Griff. I promise."

His eyes softened perceptibly, and his shoulders

seemed to relax under his tan, button front, uniform shirt.

"I kind of think we're all heading for disaster," he said, "but I'll do this your way. For now. If I can arrange it with them this evening, tomorrow I'll tell Griff I was going to help Dad fix his barn roof, and Mom clean out the attic. I'll make sure he gets there tomorrow morning, and you can take over at one, when I have to go to work. If it falls through, I'll stick around him anyway."

"Roofing in the ninety-degree heat." She couldn't help but smile at him. "Is this to help Griff reconcile with your parents, or some sort of revenge?"

He gave her the barest of smiles. "It's a guarantee that he'll hotfoot it out of here at the earliest possible convenience. And that's what we all want, isn't it?"

"Especially Griff," she agreed without really agreeing.

"Just look at it this way, Tessa. If he stays on that roof the whole time it takes to finish that job and mends the scorched bridges between himself and Dad and Mom like you want, I'd be willing to say anything could happen," Clay told her. "Just think. You could get the miracle you're looking for."

"I'm not looking for any miracle," she denied.

"Sure you are, Tessa," he said, giving her a knowing look. "We all are, when it comes to love. It's just that some of us aren't going to be in the dole. Maybe you'll get lucky."

He might be right, Tessa thought. But just like Clay, she didn't think she was in line for any more miracles. She'd gotten a second chance with Jeb, was going to hold on to that chance for dear life, and Griff would either take the opportunity she was about to hand him to reconcile with his family, or leave town. Either way, she was going to be happy.

She swore she was.

Chapter Six

Working the eight-thirty rush in the bakery the next morning, Tessa almost dropped her pencil when she saw Griff come through the door. He was supposed to be safely tied up at his parents', roofing. Something must have fallen through with that. Even so, Clay had promised to stick by him all morning until she was done working. Where was *he?*

"Hey, Tessa. Sadie around?"

"Why?"

That half curved, devilishly appealing grin of his appeared again. "You share your secrets, darlin', I'll share mine."

She would have given him a cute answer, but remembered there were customers all around eating up every word instead of focusing on her pastries. "She's in the back, Griff."

He set off through the door to the kitchen, whistling.

Frustration bubbled in her. Griff was making her nervous. It should be obvious to a dead man that she wasn't about to call off the wedding to Clay, and Griff was no corpse. In fact, he'd never looked more alive—or delicious—than in the form-fitting blue jeans and blueberry colored, short sleeve shirt he was wearing at the moment. Anyway, he had to know by now she and Clay weren't going to leave him alone so that this mysterious e-mailer could approach him, so why wouldn't he just go?

The fact that there was still some person out there who had wanted to break up her wedding added to her irritation, and she cast a suspicious gaze around the handful of customers they had. Her perusal was interrupted by her grandmother's laughter. She looked to her left.

Sadie was scurrying toward the door, and she flung her apron to Tessa as she went past her. "Griff gave me today off, too!" Sadie said merrily and, like a tiny tornado, breezed out the door.

He had? Tessa carried the apron to the back along with her orders. Griff was standing by the worktable, putting on a fresh apron, grinning from ear to ear.

"I don't think I've seen my grandmother that happy in a long time." Except for yesterday afternoon around Horace Fortune, but she wasn't going to think about that. "It was nice of you to volunteer again." She gave him a small, but genuine smile. For all she wished him gone, anyone who made Sadie happy made her happy, too.

"Glad to do it." Griff had done more than volunteer to work for Sadie. After finding out from Jasper the night before that Horace Fortune was a fine man who was trying to work up the courage to court Sadie, Griff had driven out to Horace's place and encouraged him. The man was waiting in his car outside to take Sadie out for the day. Just as Griff had expected, Sadie had jumped at the chance. He'd done it to show Tessa he did care about family, but he wasn't going to tell her that. If it all worked out well, she'd know in good time, and she would have him to thank.

Tessa knew she couldn't ask him about going to his folks' house, as she didn't know why Clay hadn't already brought him, and didn't want to give Griff any information he didn't need. So she put him to work, trying hard not to think of Griff's motivations for volunteering at a job for which he was obviously ill suited as they filled customers' orders and baked until the ten o'clock coffee club came in. By that time, they were so busy that she only nodded distractedly when Griff offered to help her serve. He unloaded the retirees' orders carefully in front of each man as she filled their coffee mugs, but then, instead of following Tessa into the kitchen, he asked for—and got—their attention.

"I'd like to ask you all a question about an e-mail I received."

Before anyone could speak, Tessa was tugging on his sleeve. "Uh, Griff, we're too busy to talk to the customers."

"Let the man speak, Tessa," Kinley Boison said. "What e-mail would that be?"

Griff scanned all five men, one by one, and nothing registered in their faces except curiosity. He would bet money no one there had contacted him. Tessa had progressed to pulling on his arm, and he purposely avoided looking at her so that the men wouldn't connect her with his questions. Instead of being grateful, she sighed and let go of him.

"Someone sent me an unsigned e-mail to get me

back here, and I'm trying to figure out who might have done it.''

"Heck, Griff, about the only ones I can think of who might want you home for a visit would be your mama and daddy,'' Jasper said. "Did you ask them?''

"Not yet.'' Griff shook his head. Turning with a "Thanks, anyway,'' he headed back to the kitchen, with Tessa on his heels. He stopped just inside the door, which she shut.

"It would be so much easier if you would just tell me what's going on,'' he said, leaning against the wall and crossing his arms over his chest. "Then you wouldn't have to have a heart attack every time I talk to anyone.''

Tessa picked up a bowl of ingredients she'd mixed before the interruption and searched for a large spoon in the drawer. "Maybe you should ask your parents about the e-mail,'' she said, trying her best to sound nonchalant but not quite sure if she succeeded, from the dark way Griff looked at her. "Really.''

She had three reasons for pushing him doing so. First, she thought it would help open up a conversation between Griff, his mom and his dad, and ease the tension Clay had told her had built up from Griff's years of neglect. Secondly, she knew they didn't know about Jeb. She was positive, because she couldn't imagine Griff's father remaining silent about that. Third, it would seclude him away from the public for a while, and give her a break. All around, getting him to go to the Ledoux's was a great idea.

"I don't think so,'' Griff said, watching the oven timer and catching it just before it was set to go off. "I've got more likely people I can think of to talk to.''

Tessa, Griff thought, was not looking happy. Not at

GET FREE BOOKS and a FREE MYSTERY GIFT WHEN YOU PLAY THE...

Just scratch off the silver box with a coin. Then check below to see the gifts you get!

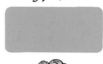

SLOT MACHINE GAME!

YES! I have scratched off the silver box. Please send me the four FREE books and mystery gift for which I qualify. I understand I am under no obligation to purchase any books, as explained on the back of this card. I am over 18 years of age.

P3KI

Mrs/Miss/Ms/Mr _____ Initials _____

BLOCK CAPITALS PLEASE

Surname _____

Address _____

_____

Postcode _____

7	7	7	**Worth FOUR FREE BOOKS plus a BONUS Mystery Gift!**
🍒	🍒	🍒	**Worth FOUR FREE BOOKS!**
♣	♣	♣	**Worth ONE FREE BOOK!**
🔔	🔔	🍒	**TRY AGAIN!**

Visit us online at www.millsandboon.co.uk

The Reader Service™ — Here's how it works:

NO STAMP NEEDED!

THE READER SERVICE™
FREE BOOK OFFER
FREEPOST CN81
CROYDON
CR9 3WZ

NO STAMP
NECESSARY
IF POSTED IN
THE U.K. OR N.I.

all. Retrieving the chocolate chip cookies from the oven, he set them on a rack to cool. Done with that, he turned and watched her for a minute. Her eyes staring down at the bowl, she was beating up the dough. She was edgy, and that had started when he'd been questioning the patrons.

She had been sticking to him like glue since he'd gotten there. That was, when Clay wasn't home.

His eyes narrowed. Moving closer to her, so close that he could feel her gasp when his bare forearm touched hers, he said quietly, "I know I asked you already, but I'm going to ask you again, and I want the truth. You didn't send that e-mail, did you, Tessa?"

"No!" she protested. "Of course not!"

"Well, what's got you beating up on that dough?"

"Nothing. I'm fine." But she wasn't. She was a nervous wreck. Initially her upset had stemmed from his being here to begin with, then from his catching her by surprise after a whole morning yesterday of his not asking any customers anything. But she'd seen the looks on all the men's faces, and they clearly hadn't known what he was talking about, so she didn't have that immediate concern that all hell was about to break loose.

No, she was beating the dough because he was confusing her so badly. One minute she was liking him all over again for making her grandmother so happy with another day off, and the next minute she would cheerfully drive him to that Air Force Base in North Carolina all by herself if that's what it would take to get him out of her life.

And then there was his being close enough now to kiss her again, and her wanting him to do that, and maybe even more, and that was especially making her nervous. She wasn't supposed to be feeling this way about him. He'd broken her heart, darn it all!

He took the bowl and spoon from her and put it aside on the worktable. "You might not have sent the e-mail, but I think there's something you're afraid of me finding out." He paused. "You don't ever have to be afraid of me, Tessa. Even if I'm not the marrying kind, there's a part of me where you're concerned that still wishes I was."

Hot tears threatened to fill her eyes. His warm hand cupped her cheek tenderly, and she blinked, hard. If she cried, he would know she was hiding something. And she couldn't risk his finding out, and maybe Clay's losing Jeb, or even herself losing Jeb, if Griff decided to raise a ruckus and take her to court for never telling him he was a father.

Griff was waiting for her answer, so she had to give him one. "I'm worried because there is someone out there who apparently wanted to come between Clay and me. And I don't want that to happen."

Griff's hand dropped to his side, and he took a step backward, his eyes registering hurt for about as long as it took him to shrug and say cynically, "Yeah. You and Clay together is probably for the best at that."

"It is," she insisted.

"Probably it would be for the best, too, if I just left and ignored any other e-mails I might get," he said, taking off his apron.

She nodded quickly. "Probably."

"Too bad, then. Because I'm not ready to go."

Later that evening, with Jeb safely in bed, Griff spent an hour dialing the phone numbers of familiar names in his brother's small black book, which held not one woman's name and number. Not even Tessa's. Probably Clay had her number memorized, but maybe not. Something was definitely wrong in the relationship. The two of them hadn't spent a minute together that they didn't have to.

There's something between them... The words in that e-mail were haunting him. Unfortunately all the old friends and acquaintances he'd called claimed to know nothing about e-mails. Most of them had nothing to do with the Internet. The way he figured it, they would have no reason not to tell him they were the mysterious e-mail sender.

His brother? Could his brother have sent it, wanting to get out of the marriage? If he had, why the sudden turn in the total opposite direction? Why not agree with Griff that it was all a bad idea and tell Tessa?

The front door opened, and Clay stepped through alone, giving Griff as good an opportunity as any to ask. He waited until his brother had changed out of his uniform, checked on Jeb and then joined him in the living room with a beer and a sack of microwave popcorn. But before he could mention the e-mail, Clay spoke.

"You want to know what else I was meaning to get done this week?"

"I couldn't imagine," Griff said, trying very hard not to think of all the possibilities. The thought of Tessa and Clay doing anything together was rubbing him like skin against cement, abrasive and shredding. He had to get them to call this wedding off. For a second, he wondered if it was jealousy he was really feeling, but it couldn't be. He wasn't about to let himself think he was in love with her. It was just the same old sexual attraction that had always been between them. Not love.

"I need you to go help Dad put the roof on his barn."

Griff pushed himself off the sofa. "No, I don't think so. That would be too much like the old days, with Dad lecturing and Mom hovering."

He turned and started into the kitchen for a beer of his own. Clay followed.

"It would give you a chance to ask Mom and Dad if they sent you that e-mail."

Clay was really pushing this. Pausing by the door of the refrigerator, he regarded his brother carefully. "You think they had something to do with that?"

Clay shrugged. "Mom was saying how much she missed you a couple weeks ago. Dad's pretty crafty. He might have come up with the idea."

"Yeah, if they quit arguing long enough."

Clay's eyebrows lifted. "Arguing?" He shook his head. "They're like two peas in a pod. Haven't heard them raise their voices around each other in years."

"What happened? Mom finally conk Dad over the head like she was always threatening?"

Clay gave a slight shake of his head. He stared at him. "I really think you should go pay them a long visit tomorrow, Griff. Dad could use the help. He's getting older now."

"I'll think about it."

"Yeah, you do that. But don't spend a long time at it. Tessa will be here at 8:00 a.m. to pick you and Jeb up. Pack his bathing suit, y'hear? Jeb likes to go swimming there." Flipping his bottle into the trash, he gave Griff a short wave of his hand. "Lock up. I'm going to bed."

"Lock up? In downtown Athens?"

Clay shrugged. "Things have changed around here in ten years, Griff. Lots of things. And people, too. You should open up your eyes, and maybe you would see. A trip to Dad and Mom's might be like a new set of glasses."

"I have twenty-twenty vision."

Clay shook his head. "You only think you do, little brother. But you can't see what's right before your eyes." With that, he disappeared into the other room, and seconds later, Griff heard his bedroom door shut down the hall.

Clay was right about at least one thing changing. Everyone in the area was getting real good at not saying things flat out. Had his brother meant that there was no real reason for him to stay there, or that there was something in plain sight that he just wasn't getting?

Damn. He guessed maybe a trip to his parents was in order to see what Clay was talking about. He supposed that he hadn't come back with any desire other than to make sure his brother and Tessa ended up happy, and he guessed he could do worse than to add a few other people to his list before he left. He'd already started with Sadie, and he did owe his parents a visit.

And an apology for not visiting more often.

It was only then he remembered that he'd been about to accuse Clay of bringing him back here. But after their conversation, he kind of doubted Clay would have been the one who e-mailed him. His brother just didn't seem all that pleased to see him.

But who, then? His parents? He doubted it, but it certainly wouldn't hurt to ask.

* * *

The next day, from atop his father's barn in the midday sun, Griff could see Jeb swimming and Tessa and his mom lounging by the aboveground pool in back of the farmhouse he'd grown up in. Five minutes more of ripping up shingles, and the hand holding his roofing ax went to his side as he found himself looking down there again, watching the way the sunlight seemed to glint off Tessa's ash-blond hair, and the way she laughed at something his mother said, and the way her gaze never seem to leave Jeb.

Jeb seemed just as attached to Tessa. When the boy got out of the pool, he came running to her instead of his grandmother to be toweled off, and then the three of them disappeared into the house for a few minutes.

It felt as if Tessa and Jeb belonged together. Maybe he was looking at this marriage the wrong way. Maybe the point wasn't whether Tessa would be happy with Clay, but whether Jeb needed Tessa in his life. Suddenly he didn't know. Another surge of guilt went through him. He was supposed to be breaking up his brother and Tess so both would be happy, but Tessa already looked exactly that when she was around Jeb—happy. Damn. Maybe she should be his nephew's mother.

Maybe he was doing the wrong thing.

"Staring ain't gonna get them back out of the house. Why don't you just take a break? Go inside and see what they're doing?"

His dad's voice startled him, and Griff almost dropped his ax. Twisted around, he half grinned at his father, Jacques. "I wasn't staring."

"You weren't ripping, either. So just what are you

doing up here with me?'' Jacques grinned back at him. ''Besides sweating?''

His father's grin gave Griff reason to pause. Jacques had always intimidated him when he'd been a teenager, but he seemed so different now, after all these years. Mellowed, Griff guessed. ''I'm here because I figured it would be a good way to let you know I'm sorry I haven't been much of a son in the past few years.''

Jacques gave him a long, searching look. ''So your brother didn't force you into coming today to help me?''

A hint of a grin came back to Griff. ''Could Clay ever force me to do anything?''

They chuckled together, and then Jacques half stepped carefully over to him, gave him a hug with one arm and then nodded.

''Apology accepted. Your mom will be pleased. You should know that despite the fact that we were sorry you left to begin with we are damned proud of you, son. If anything, we're guilty, too, of not saying that to you.''

Griff's throat felt thick with something he hadn't felt in a long time. His parents were proud of what he'd accomplished. Damn, but knowing that felt good.

''We were disappointed that we didn't see you much over the last few years, but we always understood. You were different, Griff. Your dreams always made you think there was something more and better than what you had here.''

''Can't disagree with that,'' Griff said. ''That's exactly what I thought.''

''My question is, was there?''

Griff didn't want to answer. His heart soared every time he got into a plane and flew it into the blue sky.

He couldn't deny that pleasure was worth leaving for. Still...

"More, yes. But better?" He shook his head. "I haven't found better yet, Dad."

"Probably, son, you won't." Jacques gave a long, pointed look down toward the poolside where Tessa once again had appeared with Jeb and his wife. "I think your 'better' is right down there, and, from the rumors I've been hearing, I think you came home because you knew that and wanted her back."

Griff followed his gaze. Tessa had changed into a one-piece, body skimming, apple-green swimsuit with a zipper down the front. Oh, man. His imagination went wild, his body jumped into gear and he wiped the sweat off his forehead. She hopped into the pool with Jeb, who gleefully began splashing her. Droplets of water ran all over her body, reminding him of the one time they'd spent together, down by the pond.

He'd been the one splashing water on her then, and the one whose arms had been around her, and now... well, now, he could only think about how much he envied Jeb.

Jacques started walking back to where he'd been yanking up the roof, piece by piece, and pulled his arm across his forehead to wipe off the sweat.

"So *are* you fixing to claim what's been yours all these years while you're home, son?"

Griff shook his head and wiped beads of his own sweat off that he wasn't sure were so much from the heat, after staring at Tessa. "It wouldn't work for us. Nothing's changed since we broke up."

"Are you sure about that?"

"Why? You know something about Tessa that I don't?" His gaze traveled to his dad at the same time his gut tightened. Jacques was getting at something, but what? Didn't any of his family speak plain English anymore?

"Your mother said it seems kind of obvious that Tessa is settling for second best in her life." Jacques paused to pull up a shingle and then throw it off the side of the roof onto the large hauler behind his tractor. "It's not Clay she wants to marry, it's the ready-made family."

"How do we know that?"

Jacques stared at him. "*We* know that? Sounds like you agree, you just don't know why."

"I do agree. So tell me the why."

Bending down, Jacques started working again. "First and foremost, you broke up that wedding pretty danged easy, and she didn't come running back to Clay the second you put her down on her feet after you carried her off. I don't think that marriage could have been stopped if Tessa hadn't subconsciously had her doubts."

His father had a point. She could have run back to the church at any time, she could have opened that door to the sanctuary the second she saw him and run to Clay, she could have calmly walked over to the phone in Casey's Kitchen and called Clay when they'd arrived. Instead she had focused in on him.

"Then, here today, Tessa touched you on the shoulder when she passed by you, and she's been glancing up here about as much as you've been staring down there. Whenever she comes here with Clay, she doesn't pay him a lick of attention. Her eyes are all for Jeb."

"I noticed that."

"Do you still have romantic feelings for her?"

Griff stared at his father, surprised Jacques would

ask such a personal question. His father did seem a little embarrassed, staring down at his work instead of meeting Griff's eyes. But Griff liked it. The concern showed his father cared, really cared. Probably he always had, but now he was showing it. A pleasant sense of belonging, of love of family, flooded through Griff.

It felt great.

"It doesn't matter what feelings either of us have, Dad," he said with a long whoosh of breath from his lungs. "We weren't meant for each other. She needs to stay here, and I need…" He paused, searching for words that could express what he needed.

"The *more* we just finished talking about?"

"I guess." Truthfully Griff wasn't sure what he needed. He set about working on the roof again with a vengeance, as though hard work would point him in the right direction.

"The only advice I can give you about Tessa is not to put blinders on where she's concerned."

Griff carefully put his ax on the roof, starting to feel a little exasperated. "Clay said the same thing to me last night about my trip home in general. I wish I knew what you all were talking about."

"She's a grown woman now. Maybe she can see more clearly what she wants—if you're still willing to give it to her."

"You're saying you think she would come with me?"

Jacques put down his own tool and stood. "I'm only saying to take a good look at what the 'more' is that you could have, that you don't have now." He gestured toward the ladder. "Let's go down and take a break, and you can mull it over a piece."

He joined his father by the ladder, but then stopped to ask him something.

"Did you and Mom send me an e-mail with the wedding particulars on it to get me home?"

"I heard you were asking that around town." Jacques shook his head. "Not us, son. But if you find out who did it, let me know. I want to shake the hand of whoever got you back in our lives again."

All the way down the ladder and over to the pool, out of which Tessa was climbing, Griff thought about what his father had said. About the "more" he could have. Could he and Tessa make a relationship between them work now? There was still attraction between the two of them—strong, spellbinding attraction. But did he love her as she was now, or was his wanting her in his life a desire based only on memories of the way things had been? He couldn't answer that. There was also still the fact that his life on the road and the flying, with the excitement that entailed, he still needed, and she claimed to hate. So what the hell did he have to offer her anyway?

A child. The thought came like a crystal clear bolt of lightning, and he stopped where he was near the pool. He could offer her a baby of her own. Nothing in his mind could accept that she loved Clay—he had seen Tessa in love, and she wasn't acting like it now. So Jeb had to be the attraction in this marriage. If all she wanted was to be a mother—would that be enough for her? Would she go with him if he told her he wanted a child?

Did he want a child?

Tessa seemed to appear before him like a vision. "Griff, I asked you if you wanted—"

He froze.

"Water?" She held out a glass.

Oh, yeah, he wanted water. He took the tumbler she offered, leaned over and poured the cold water over his head, drowning his unruly thoughts in it. A baby. He had to be crazy. Crazy with lust.

Shaking his head and then straightening, he palmed the water out of his short, military style cut and handed the glass back to her. "Thanks."

"That's one way to get the water in you," Tessa said, her mouth lifting sideways in a smile. "Let it soak in through your head."

"Griff never took the easy road," his mother, Mary, said, showing up at Tessa's side with a pitcher of ice tea.

Griff couldn't seem to move. His dad had said to take the blinders off, and it was like he was looking at Tessa through new eyes. She stood in sleek blondness, having pulled on one of those calf-length, bathing suit cover-up skirts that was slit up the side and slinking down over her hips. He wanted to touch her, pull her close and get her alone, and it was the last thing either of them needed.

"Your father said you had a water jug up on the roof." Mary took the glass, filled it with tea, and smiled. "When I heard you were coming, I had Jeb get one of Clay's swim trunks and bring it along. Why don't you take a dip in the pool with Tessa and Jeb before lunch?"

Jeb nodded enthusiastically. "I'll let you play with my boat, Uncle Griff."

"Can't turn down an offer like that." He turned to Tessa. "How about you, Tessa?"

"You're welcome to join us, but I've got nothing for you to play with," she said wryly, almost to warn him. She scooted over to the ladder, where she hurriedly pulled off the skirt she wore and tossed it over the back of a nearby chair.

Truth be told, she didn't really want to go back in the water; she wanted to flee home to the safety of her upstairs apartment, away from Griff. Something had changed for him up on the roof. There had been a new level of tension between them when their eyes had met seconds ago. He'd seemed to be searching her face for some sign, what of, she didn't know. It couldn't be about Jeb because his parents didn't know the truth and couldn't have told him, but still—something had to have been said up there.

And something was going to happen between them before he left again; she could feel it all the way to her toes. She wanted him. She wanted him with a depth of passion that she couldn't remember ever feeling.

Climbing onto a plastic raft, she floated and watched her secret son playing with a yellow, toy snorkel. He surfaced with a sunshiny smile. She started to smile back, but then realized he wasn't looking at her.

"Jump!" Jeb yelled.

Just as her head started to turn to see whom Jeb was talking to, a mini tidal wave of water covered her, and then she and her raft tipped right into the spot next to her where Griff had belly flopped. In seconds, she felt her flesh pressed against Griff's warm, wet body and, given the nature of her suit's material, she might as well have been naked. A surge of desire went through her, and she almost reached out to pull him closer. Before she could, though, he was hoisting her up out of the water in his arms. She clung to his neck for dear life.

"Look what I caught, Jeb!"

Jeb collapsed in giggles. "A whale!"

Tessa sputtered. "Jeb Ledoux, you're going to be *so* sorry when I catch you."

Griff easily hoisted her higher. "No, Jeb, not a whale. She's as light as a feather. You want me to drop her and see if she floats?"

All too aware of her how hot her body was becoming where it was pressed into Griff's, Tessa reached over to right where she knew his vulnerable spot was about two inches above his waist and tickled him.

"Hey!" He dropped her feet into the water and stepped back from her, a fake pout on his lips. "I can't have any fun."

"That'll teach you to pick me up!" she told him, giggling.

"Pick her up again, Uncle Griff," Jeb called out from the other side of the pool. "Throw her into the water."

"Not unless he wants more like you're going to get," she said, lunging forward for the child, picking him up and putting him on the raft. She tickled him on his belly as they both laughed from deep inside of them. The laugh of the carefree.

And it had been Griff who started it.

With that thought, her hand dropped down to rest on the raft. Seizing his opportunity, Jeb rolled off the other side into the water, but that was all right. Turning, she sliced her hand through the water and splashed Griff, right when he wasn't expecting it.

He yelped and started splashing her back. Jeb joined in, and pretty soon the three of them were having water fights using a toy bucket, water pistols, and the oldest method of all—hanging on to the side of the pool and kicking with their feet to drench each other.

"Y'all can get out of the pool and come and eat," Mary called from the patio table, where she had laid out sandwiches, chips and drinks.

"Aw, Mamaw!" Jeb said.

"Aw, Ma!" Griff echoed.

"I, for one, will be happy to get out of this mess of men," Tessa said, laughing again as she started to climb the ladder.

"Did you hear what she called us, Jeb?" Griff asked. "She called us messy men!"

"Let's get her!" Jeb's voice rang out.

Tessa glanced over her shoulder to see Griff opening his arms to grab her, and she kicked backward, splashing him. He grabbed her foot, and she was giggling so hard she pushed away, let go and slid into the water. The next thing she knew, he had grabbed her and picked her up again into his arms, and she was laughing and sputtering, and when her eyes cleared, all she saw was his face, so near to hers her breath caught. They gazed at each other as though they were the only two people in the world, and Tessa thought he was going to kiss her. She wished he would. His lips got closer, and she closed her eyes, and forgot everything else...

And then Jeb's call stopped both of them cold.

"Daddy!"

Chapter Seven

The adoring, gleeful greeting coming from Jeb for his adopted father hit Tessa hard, shattering the crystal-beautiful world that had been hers in the pool and reminding her of what really was her whole world—becoming Jeb's mother, Griff or no Griff. Sloshing past them, the child at stake climbed out of the pool and ran toward Clay.

"We didn't do anything," Griff whispered consolingly as he put her back on her feet.

"Not even what was right," she told him, trying to regain her composure and mentally ice over the heat in her limbs that had come from rubbing bodies with Griff again. Climbing out of the pool, she saw Mary catch her grandson and wrap a towel around him before he hugged his father, who was in uniform. Quickly drying herself off and slipping her cover-up back on, she walked into the house barefoot, slipping past Clay, who moved aside to avoid touching her. In the front room, she figured they wouldn't be overheard by those still outside, and she waited there. Just as she thought he would, Clay followed.

"Nothing happened," she told him the second he entered the room.

Clay's gaze, for a change, settled on her. "Maybe you'd better think on that for a while."

"We're still getting married, right?" They *had* to get married. Jeb needed her. She needed him. "Our first priority is still Jeb, isn't it?"

His chest expanding with a deep breath, Clay opened his mouth to say something, shut it and shook his head slowly, and a sense of dread filled her. "Maybe you should tell me what you really want, Tessa."

"To be Jeb's mother," she said, but her voice shook a little. "I really want that more than anything."

"Or anyone?" Clay's long look told her he thought otherwise, but then he sighed. "You might want to redouble your efforts to get Griff to leave, then, because it was obvious to everyone who saw you and Griff together that there's something going on between you two, whether you want to admit it or not. And that's not good for my son to see, not if you're still planning on being his new mama."

He walked out. Through the picture window, she watched him get into his police unit and drive away, and she dabbed at her eyes to hold back her tears.

Clay was correct. Either her feelings for Griff were being newly aroused, or she had never quite lost them to begin with. Whichever the case, showing them to everyone wasn't right. It could only confuse Jeb. She couldn't let emotions rule her life, as they had her father's. He'd never had a minute's peace—and neither

had she, as his daughter. Almost kissing Griff today
had been an emotional act, and staying away from him
from this point on would be the right thing to do. Just
as getting him to leave town so he would never find
out he was Jeb's father from anyone was the right thing
to do.

She knew it was—she'd just let herself slip for a
minute there. Seeing Clay's irritation had reminded her
of just how much she stood to lose if she gave in to
her emotions once more where Griff was concerned,
and she wouldn't forget again.

Griff considered getting into the middle of whatever
Clay was discussing with Tessa, but it was none of his
business. He did realize Clay had probably guessed he
had been about to kiss Tessa in the pool—certainly his
mother and father had. Even while smiling for Jeb's
sake, their eyes mirrored their disapproval. Having already eaten, his father took off toward the barn again,
alone. His mother, after she got Jeb squared away out
of earshot at a child's size picnic table, sat down next
to him.

"I guess I just wore out my welcome in Claiborne
Landing," Griff said to her.

"I've seen better timing on cheap watches," she acknowledged, reaching over and grabbing a sandwich
off the serving platter. "Eat. When you're done, you
can join your father back up on the roof—away from
Tessa."

"Okay."

"Good. It'll appease him. And to appease me, you
can come clean with just what you thought you were
doing in the pool."

Griff managed to eat half of his ham and cheese on a hard roll before he came up with something to say.

"I don't rightly know," he admitted. He studied her and the way she'd fixed her black hair in stylish waves around her face. "You don't look a day older than when I left for school, Mom. How did you manage that?"

His mother laughed. "Amazing how the more trouble you boys get into, the prettier I get." She drank some tea, wiped her lips with a paper napkin and leaned forward. "But all the compliments in the world aren't going to lift you off the hook that easily. If you two are still in love, why on earth did you break up years ago?"

He filled her in on Tessa's miserable childhood. "The third year I was away, Tessa told me she was happy right here, that this was her home, and she was never going to leave it or her grandmother. Nor was she going to spend her days alone in some strange city while I worked, having to rebuild her life every time I got restationed. That didn't fit in with what I'd spent all that time training for."

"And you weren't going to give up your dream of flying, not even for love."

Griff wished his mother hadn't said it so bluntly. He shifted uncomfortably. "Flying is all I ever wanted."

"And having a family and a home that she never had to leave must be all Tessa ever wanted," Mary countered. "I guess I can understand why she wants to marry Clay, then."

She fell silent for a minute, eating, but then her eyes squinted. "But that doesn't make sense," she said, almost to herself. "If she wanted to stay right here, and even broke up with you over it, the man she obviously is still in love with, whether she knows it or not—why on earth did she then spend a year in Dallas?''

Griff put down his drink and stared at her. As his mother gave him the details, how Tessa had needed to get away after their breakup and then stayed to help Lindy with Jeb, something inside him twisted, tightly. His mother had asked a danged good question, he thought, one that he was going to ask Tessa at his earliest possible convenience.

That afternoon, Tessa took Jeb and Griff home, and to be honest, he was too worn-out from roofing to confront her about Dallas. Besides, Jeb was right there, sitting between them. The following three mornings, he drove Jeb to the farm straight from Clay's, and Tessa went to work, and he didn't even see her until she showed up in the afternoons to spend a couple of hours with Jeb. He was too busy trying to help his father to really talk to her, although he found himself watching her whenever he could.

He had a tense feeling in his gut that was building to an ache. She could go to Dallas for a year, but she couldn't even try to leave with him? What the hell had that been all about?

Tessa went home each day before he finished work, leaving him to bring Jeb home and feed him supper. It was as if she was still keeping an eye on him, but avoiding him at the same time. He could understand her staying away after what had almost happened in the pool—obviously she'd realized she was risking her chances of marrying Clay. But nevertheless, he wanted answers about Dallas, and he became determined to confront her so he could get them.

The evening before the "Welcome Back, Griff" barbecue, as his mother had termed it, Sadie called him, said she had a surprise planned for the next day and asked him to stick around town for another day or so. He had no idea why she wanted him to stay, but there was something he'd learned long ago growing up in Louisiana—when an older lady asked you to do something, you obeyed. With respect. He just hoped it wasn't some matchmaking scheme. He wasn't in the mood right then.

The next morning, he went to Tessa's apartment, only to find out from Sadie that she'd already left for his parents' farm to help his mother out.

"Talk some sense into her, Griff," Sadie called from her own, half-open door.

"Yes, ma'am," he agreed. "But about what?"

"You know," Sadie said. He had barely registered that she seemed to be in an awful hurry, when she gave him a quick, cheery wave of her fingertips and closed the door.

Another mystery. From there, he went over to his parents' farm where he found his brother and nephew outside admiring the roofing job, and, seizing his chance, he went inside to find Tessa, get her alone, and make her explain about Dallas. After that, his only plan was to set a time to leave town, because he really thought he'd go crazy if he didn't go soon. The odd jobs weren't pushing him away—he'd enjoyed the novelty and the way he'd felt as if he was fitting into his family and community again, even though his brother

was keeping his emotional distance. No, it was Tessa.
It had always been Tessa keeping him away.

Standing next to Mary, chopping celery for a mac-
aroni salad for the barbecue at noon, Tessa saw Griff
coming up to the back door. The past three days of
seeing him but barely speaking to him had been terrible, but necessary. She knew Clay was right. Jeb
couldn't be exposed to anything like she'd almost exposed him to. Every time she was close to Griff, she
wanted him all over again, even though she knew it
could never work between them, and she was worried
about controlling herself. So she stayed away.

She dropped her knife onto the cutting board. "I'll
be upstairs looking at those toys you wanted me to go
through."

"We aren't done here—" Mary protested, but
stopped when she saw the stricken expression on
Tessa's face. Tessa hurriedly wiped her hands, took off
her apron and tossed it toward a chair on her way out
of the kitchen. As she entered the hallway, she heard
the back door open, but she didn't stop until she was
in Griff's old room, standing next to the bed and looking down at a large cardboard box marked Griff's
Toys. Mary had asked her two days ago to sort through
them for any Jeb might want to keep. The rest would
be going to charity. But because they had been Griff's,
and because she'd be giving them to his child, Tessa
had been reluctant to tackle the task.

She picked up a fire truck that, except for the dust,
was in excellent shape, for being over twenty years old.

"I never played with that."

She spun around, surprised his mother had told him

where she was. In fact, she was shocked Mary would even let him up the stairs near her after having witnessed them nearly kissing. She held the truck in her hands, not knowing what to say.

"I never went through a fireman stage, so I kept it on top of that dresser." He stepped inside the room and indicated the bare oak dresser behind her. "Some kid would probably really like it."

Some kid...like his own son. She held it to her almost protectively and regarded him with a tiny smile, trying to act as though nothing at all was bothering her about being there, in his bedroom by his bed, alone with him, with part of his past in her hand, and with his almost kiss on her mind. "I think Jeb would love it. He adores fire trucks."

"You spend a lot of time with him, so I guess you would know." He shrugged and stepped closer to her, so that they were shoulder to shoulder, making her all the more aware of him—as if she needed any help.

He had dressed up a bit for his "Welcome back" barbecue, with a green sports shirt and tailored, tan trousers. As he leaned forward to shift around the toys in the box, the way his shirt went snug against his back made her desperately want to trace the lines of his muscles with her fingertips. She gripped the fire truck more tightly to keep herself from touching him.

Fishing a model World War II airplane out of the box, he lit up with that half-curved grin of his that always made her feel a little dizzy. He looked like Jeb on Christmas morning. "My P-51. I thought this was gone forever. I made it in the third grade when I started studying everything I could about planes."

"But you would have only been about eight. You

knew you wanted to be a pilot that early?'' She hadn't even been thinking about the future when she was that age, just surviving the present.

He nodded, studying the details of the plane as though seeing it for the first time. Then he put it down on the white chenille bedspread and examined her with the same intensity he'd used on his toy. ''Speaking of the past, I came up here to ask why it was so easy for you to leave Claiborne Landing for Dallas, when you couldn't even try to leave for me.''

Tessa froze. What to say? Who had told him? The e-mailer? Did Griff now know about Jeb? No. He couldn't, or he would have said it right out.

''Tessa? I want an answer on this one.''

Keep it simple, she told herself. She leaned forward and pulled something else from the box. ''I needed to get away after we broke up.''

''There has to be more to it than that,'' Griff said. She wasn't looking him in the eyes, and she seemed shaken. ''Why did you stay away so long?''

She straightened up, but her focus was on his old catcher's mitt.

''I was visiting Lindy and Clay, and then she asked for my help after Jeb was born, and so I stayed until they returned here.'' She put the catcher's mitt down alongside the fire truck. ''I always intended on coming back, but for a time, it was easier to be away.''

Reaching out, Griff gently turned her to face him. For a second their eyes met, and held, and he read all kinds of wishes and hopes in them, or thought he did. But then her face masked over, and she left his side to go to the window and gazed down at the yard. ''People are arriving for the picnic. We should go downstairs.''

"Not yet. What do you mean it was easier to be away?" he asked, and the question made her turn around again.

"Griff, of all people, I figured you'd be the one person who would already know the answer to that."

She had a point. He took a deep breath. "I feel like there's a wall between us since Clay caught us almost kissing."

"Of course there is. I shouldn't have forgotten I'm getting married to someone else."

"It's not that, and you know it."

He saw a flash of guilt in her eyes. But it fled swiftly and was replaced by irritation. "The wall really went up," she said pointedly, "a long time ago when I figured out you didn't love me."

"Of course I loved you," he said, opening his palms in frustration that she could believe he hadn't.

"Love is putting the other person first over your own desires. You didn't."

"Neither did you." He'd been so angry when she'd called off their engagement and told him not to bother her anymore, as though she'd never mattered to him. He'd thought he'd gotten over that feeling a long time ago, but it was all flooding back now. Reminded of his father's former, automatic responses to just about everything that annoyed him, Griff purposely worked on quelling it.

"You knew what my dreams were from the moment you met me," he said evenly, but his jaw was tense. "I never changed. You always acted like what I wanted was what you wanted, too."

"I wanted you to be happy." She thought back. "The closer we got to getting married, the more I realized how much I needed to have a place to call home, with friends and family there. You have no idea how horrible it was growing up always worrying about where you were going next. Knowing not to make friends, not to get close to anyone, because you'd move, and they'd be left behind. If I left with you, that's how it would have been, and I wasn't ready for that."

"Then how did you survive Dallas?"

"I knew that it was temporary. That I was helping Lindy, and that we'd all be going back home to Claiborne Landing—together. I knew they would be there for me, Griff. But with you, moving away wouldn't be temporary, and I would be alone while you were flying. All alone."

"It wouldn't be as bad as you're painting it, Tess, and I told you that. I think the problem was more like you didn't trust me to always be there for you because your parents weren't. You figured I'd go off one day and never come back, just like your father did, and you'd be left alone again."

His blunt statement stopped Tessa cold. He was right. She wouldn't go away with him then because she hadn't trusted him and his love.

"Did you and Sadie ever find out what happened to your father?" Griff asked.

She nodded, looking down at the pool where Jeb was having fun splashing a couple of his cousins. "He had a friend send a letter apologizing to me after he passed away. I was an afterthought even in his death."

"I'm not him, Tessa—you matter to me. You always have."

This was so hard to hear. Tessa closed her eyes briefly, but it didn't make any of the pain go away.

"You know," Griff added, shrugging off what seemed to be a heavy weight on his shoulders. "I've been trying to figure out exactly what I thought I was doing by running here. I wanted to tell myself it was to save you from a marriage you really didn't want. I still don't think you want the marriage—I think you just want to be a mother."

Tessa's gaze flew to meet his, her breath held.

"Am I right?" he asked. "*Is* that why you're marrying Clay—to be a mother? Is that what you really want? What about real love?"

She walked over to sink down on the bed. The movement sent the fire truck rolling onto the carpet with a thump, but neither of them moved to pick it up. Her gaze was locked on him. What did she really want? She wanted what she'd always wanted, to have Griff and her—and their son—together as one family in Claiborne Landing, her forever home. But that wasn't a choice.

"Yes, I want to be Jeb's mother," she said softly, dropping her gaze to where her hand was smoothing the dark green ivy pattern on her skirt.

Regret and hurt settled deep within Griff. A small part of him had hoped she would say she wanted him, but of course, she hadn't. He was a fool for coming back and getting all involved with her again.

He had to get out of there. With a sweep of his hand, he indicated the toys. "As far as I'm concerned, feel free to give these all away. I doubt if Jeb would want any of his uncle's old junk and I don't see myself ever having any kids, so I don't see the point of dragging it all with me wherever I go. Besides, it's easier to forget the past without it staring me in the face reminding me of everything I left behind." Turning, he walked out of the room.

Feeling sick with guilt, Tessa stuck his truck, mitt and plane back in the box and moved it into the closet. Griff wasn't going to have any more children, ever. He would never know the exquisite pleasure of being a daddy to his son. And it was all her doing.

She swallowed, hard, as she gazed around Griff's old room. She had to pull herself together, go outside and pretend to be Clay's happy fiancée. She was doing the right thing keeping Jeb secret. She had to believe that. But she also knew, without a doubt, that the look of resignation on Griff's face when he'd said what he did about never having children was going to haunt her forever.

Sitting next to Clay in a neon purple lawn chair someone had brought, Tessa was trying to play at being Clay's fiancée. Even though her heart wasn't in it, the multitude of guests who had been invited expected it and she didn't want rumors to start that might get back to Jeb through playmates via their parents. Also, mindful the person was still out there who had summoned Griff back to town and might know about Jeb, she was keeping an eye on whoever might approach Griff who hadn't already had a chance to talk to him. She doubted anyone would give him such big news in the middle of a picnic, but nevertheless, the possibility was keeping her edgy.

"So, Clay, when's the wedding been rescheduled

to?'' Jasper asked from his chair near his wife. Reba frowned at him and pinched his arm.

''What!'' Jasper protested, yanking his arm away. ''It's a logical question to ask 'em, considering Sadie ain't around for you to ask her and tell me.''

People within earshot snickered, but Tessa sat up straight. She'd been so wrapped up with her own life, she'd totally forgotten to look for Sadie, who was not with her best friend as usual. ''Where is Grandma, Miss Reba?''

Reba, for once without her cat, gave a single wave of her hand. ''I'm not telling,'' she warbled. ''Sadie told me she would call you and that I was not to tell.''

''Maybe Griff knows,'' Clay suggested. ''Sadie called him at the house yesterday evening.''

''She did?'' Tessa frowned. Her gaze flew back to Griff, and she examined him as he talked to some old friends of his from high school. Surely he would have mentioned it this morning if something was up with her grandmother. ''What about?''

Clay shrugged. ''You'll probably have to ask Sadie.''

''I'll do that. I'm going to call her on her cell phone.'' With one more look at the pool to make sure Jeb was okay amid the laughing, splashing youngsters, she rose. ''I'll be back. Watch Jeb?''

''I never stop,'' Clay told her. His gaze on her, he added, ''He's in the pool, with Harry Jr. and Brandy on one side, and the twins on the other, and he's got his snorkel on. Yellow. Green stripes.''

She had to look to confirm his details, and then she flashed Clay a little smile right before turning to walk to the house. He was an excellent father. The best. *Just like Griff would have been.* But she couldn't think about that anymore, or she'd cry, and how would *that* look?

Fishing her phone out of her purse she'd stuck behind the living-room couch, she tapped out the numbers.

"Hello? Hello?" It was the way Sadie always answered the cell phone, because the mouthpiece didn't reach all the way down to her mouth, and she didn't think anyone could hear her.

"Grandma, you're late to the Ledoux's picnic," Tessa said. "Are you okay?"

"Of course I am. There's a good reason I'm late, dear." Sadie's voice was cheerful. "It's my surprise!"

"Your surprise is that you aren't coming?"

"My surprise is that I'm eloping to Vegas with Horace Fortune!"

Tessa closed her eyes and counted to ten.

"Hello? Hello?"

"I'm still here." In the Twilight Zone. This could not be happening to her. "Grandma, you never talked this over with me."

A merry round of laughter rang out. "Sorry. I didn't read that part in the *Bringing up Granddaughter Manual* about having to discuss every little decision I made with you."

"Marriage is hardly a little decision!"

"I know it isn't," Sadie said. "Look at all the trouble you've had with it."

"I am not under discussion here."

"You should be. You're about to marry the wrong man, and you won't even admit it. I knew you always loved Griff and never stopped, but you never want me to interfere—"

"Grandma, I can't talk about that right now." Tessa could feel her face going red with irritation. "Are you driving?"

"Goodness no. Horace won't let me. He says I speed."

The man had one good quality, at least. "I want you and Horace to turn that car around right now and come home."

"We're in his RV. After we get married, we're going to tour the West."

"Without even telling me?"

"I was going to call," Sadie said. "Now, I want you to do something for me. Take over my half of the bakery. Goodness knows you deserve it...you've worked hard all these years for it. I'll send you power of attorney."

"You can't give up your livelihood. How are you and Horace going to live?" she said weakly.

"Horace has old money."

"You mean he's from a long line of wealth?"

"No, I mean he's been stashing money in his mattress since 1950. Of course I mean his family's rich. Oil wells, that sort of thing."

"Oh, Grandma."

"Young lady, you sound pitiful. Buck up. This is going to work out better for both you and me. I've got to admit, I've been kind of lonely for a while for male companionship. And you're all grown up. You have a life to lead and you won't do it with me around. Now maybe you'll come to your senses, work things out with Griff, and go wherever will make that poor boy happy.''

Tessa sat up straight. "I can't leave."

"You only think you can't. But I notice you didn't protest about not loving him, which is exactly what I thought. Anyway, we're about to stop for lunch, so I'm going to turn this thing off. Be sure and tell Griff thank you. If he hadn't stepped in and encouraged Horace to make his move, I'd still be worshipping him from afar instead of going off to be a bride.''

She rose to her feet. "Griff did this?"

"Bye, dear!"

"Grandma?" She was talking to dead air. Snapping the cell phone closed, she considered redialing her grandmother, but she had a feeling she'd be wasting her time. Her grandmother would not be coming back, and from the sounds of it, it was all Griff's doing. He'd done nothing but cause havoc in her life since he'd returned.

It was time, she thought, to put an end to his interference once and for all.

Chapter Eight

"Ooooeee, Griff, looks like a fighter approaching at six o'clock, and she's got guns blazing." Jasper chortled.

Tessa paid him no mind. Her focus was on the man in the middle of Jasper and Reba. "You got Sadie married! How could you!" she asked, sticking her finger in his chest.

He caught her hand in his and held on. "Whoa. I don't have the power to make weddings happen—"

"No, just to stop them," she blurted back, pulling her hand free and resting it on her hip. "So how come you didn't stop Sadie's? How come you felt like you could just come back here after all this time, interfere and tear my life apart like this? Isn't it obvious that I've been trying all week to get you bored enough here so that you would just leave and get *out* of my life? Couldn't you have just gotten the hint?"

Griff's expression lost any easygoingness it had. He

would have said something right there to her about hurting his parents' feelings—they couldn't have missed hearing every word—but he didn't figure that should be a party discussion, so he took her arm and spirited her off to the other side of the barn, where they could talk in privacy.

"So that's what was behind all these odd jobs. You figured I would remember what it was about Claiborne Landing that made me want to leave to begin with."

"The lack of excitement and the boring work," she said, her jaw setting as she looked up at him.

"Now I'd call *that* devious."

"Only if it had worked. Which it didn't. Instead you took the opportunity to find someone to lure my grandmother away and make me lose the only real family I ever had."

"That wasn't the intention I had when I encouraged Horace to ask Sadie out." Because he could not stand near her without wanting to touch her, he backed up to put a little distance between them and leaned against the barn. "And if you and Clay hadn't dreamed up this crazy scheme to drive me away, I wouldn't have been in the bakery shop to arrange anything."

"This is all my own fault." Tessa paced, then stopped, close to tears, her back to Griff. Just like her father, Sadie hadn't even said goodbye. Hadn't discussed leaving with her. Just went out the door one morning and never looked back. Didn't anyone in her life care about keeping family together anymore?

She felt Griff's hand cup her shoulder. "As upset as you are, you should know your scheme did do something good. You proved to me how much I care about my family and yours. That's why I set up your grandmother with someone she could love. I didn't want her to leave you, Tess. I just wanted her to be happy. Same as I want you to be happy.''

Tessa slowly turned around and gazed upward. There was sincerity in Griff's eyes. Had he changed in his short time here? Had he come to realize what was really important?

''But Griff, she's risking a lot going off with some man she barely knows.''

''At least,'' he added, ''she was willing to take a risk.''

''Unlike me, you mean.''

He nodded. ''You're afraid of taking any risks. There's no risk in marrying Clay. Your marriage can't ever fail since it wouldn't be a marriage to begin with.''

She didn't want a marriage to Clay—she just wanted Jeb. But she couldn't tell Griff that. She didn't know whether to cry or scream with frustration.

''I made,'' she said slowly, ''and am making, the best decisions I can and I don't deserve to have you criticizing me about my choices. You always did exactly what you wanted without a second thought. It didn't matter if I needed you or not.''

''When was our relationship a question of need, Tessa? You always said you didn't need me, just wanted me, remember?''

That had been true, right up to the point when she'd been pregnant with Jeb. She clamped her lips together for a few seconds, realizing she'd almost gone too far.

''Since you didn't want to risk my being there for you, I honestly don't know what I could have changed on my part,'' Griff said. ''If we'd stayed together then, we would have made each other miserable. But now…''

"Now?" she asked warily, her fingers gripping her skirt.

"Now I understand what you were worried about missing—the feeling of being in the midst of family and community, of belonging. I didn't realize how important it was until I lived without family—and you— all these years, but I do now. If I had any hope I could make you happy, I would propose and spend the rest of my life putting you first. That's what I want now. You.''

She stared at him, numb. "Griff—''

"No, wait." He held up his hand. "I think that's subconsciously why I've been trying so hard to get you to change your mind about marrying Clay. I want you back. But there's that wall between us, Tessa, and I have no idea still why it's there.''

The wall was Jeb. Tessa bit her bottom lip. Here, at her feet, was her dream—Griff's love—back again like a gift more precious than anything. Anything, that was, besides being a mother to her baby.

But she wanted to take what he was offering her. She wanted it so badly.

"Tell me what is really going on with you. Let me be a part of your life again. I've never stopped loving you, and there's nothing here for you that I can't give you—and that includes a child of our own.''

A child? He was ready to have a child? Good Lord, what should she do? The emotional part of her was urging her to go to him, but the rational part of her was thinking that she was only going to let herself in for more heartache if she got involved with Griff on this level all over again.

But she wanted to. Lord above, she wanted to.

He reached out, and she went into his arms, unable to help herself, and he leaned down and kissed her tenderly. Her arms slipped up to circle his neck and she held on to him as if he was her lifeline. For precious seconds while he held her close, she remembered what loving him with all her heart, and no reservations, had been like, and she let herself dream again. She wished it was years ago, before her decision to give Jeb up, before everything had been set to the course it was on. But the laughter from the party reminded her that Jeb was only a few dozen yards away, and calling someone else "Daddy."

"We belong together, Tessa. Nothing I've seen in the world compares to how I feel every time I walk into a room and you're there. I'll never be totally happy without you in my life."

Pulling away, she looked up at him with tears in her eyes. "I don't know what to do. I have to think."

He nodded solemnly. "I've got some vacation left and I'll stay until you make up your mind. If what you decide you want is marriage to Clay, then I'll stop interfering. But if you do choose him, Tessa, I'll have to know why and I won't leave until I find out."

She didn't know if the last seemed like a threat, or very fair. "How do we know we aren't going to make each other miserable?"

Giving a quick glance around to make sure no one was watching them, he pulled her into his arms and kissed her again, this time a slow, deep kiss that made her forget where she was and what their problems were for long seconds. Just as they parted lips, with her arms still around his neck, he lifted her into his arms and started spinning her around. She felt lighter than air, and laughed, clinging to him and hoping he didn't land them both in the grass.

"Put me down!" she said, giggling. "Griff, what are you doing?"

"Showing you what it's like to fly." He slowed and stopped. Still holding her, he gazed into her eyes and kissed her again, until she felt breathless with desire.

"I see why you like flying so much," she said.

"You were worried we'd be miserable together. Do you feel miserable?" he asked, putting her down.

She shook her head back and forth, sending locks of ash-blond hair over her shoulders.

"Do you believe I've changed?"

She nodded.

"Then what do you say? Marry me?"

Oh, how she wanted to. The past aside, she'd missed having Griff in her life with all her heart. He made her laugh. Her cares and worries all seemed lessened with him there. But there was Jeb. She couldn't abandon her baby.

"I have to think, Griff," she said, her voice feather soft.

"So go and think. I'll be at the barbecue."

She left Griff and found Clay, telling him she was going to check that the bakery doors were locked. He frowned as though he knew she were lying, but as usual he didn't say anything to stop her. It was a good thing, because she needed to be alone to make what could well be the most important decision of her life.

Whether or not she should—or could—give up Jeb for a second time.

* * *

She ran to the one place she could always find comfort since she'd come to Claiborne Landing—Sadie's bakery. The place where the two of them had worked together, laughed together, and cried buckets of tears together. Only now, her grandmother had moved onto a new life of her own and Tessa had to cry alone.

Dabbing at her eyes with a tissue, she gazed around the familiar furnishings, wondering if she could give up what she knew and loved so well. Her heart told her in no uncertain terms that Griff had changed—his caring so much about his parents and her grandmother had proven that. He'd even proven he was putting her first, offering to walk away and let her marry Clay in peace.

Though if she did marry Clay, Griff *had* also said he wasn't leaving until he found what she was hiding. It felt as if he was still trying to have things go his way. But if the situation was reversed and she felt with all her heart that Griff was keeping something very important from her, wouldn't she have declared the same thing?

Yes, she would have. So Griff was sincere. She wanted to take a risk that she was different and could go with him wherever he went in the Air Force, so he would be happy. But that would mean leaving their child behind. That's what her father and mother had done to her, although each for different reasons, and she couldn't abandon Jeb.

Could she? More tears fell, for the first time, for the little girl she'd been who had been left behind by a mother who had had no choice, and a father who had made the wrong one. She finally understood what her mother had been going through. She hadn't been able to choose between her husband and her child, either, and she'd just done what she'd thought was best for both.

Once Tessa's tears were dried, she knew she had to do the same for her little boy as she had done years ago when he was born—make the best choice.

If she married Clay, she didn't think Griff would rest until he found out why she'd chosen his brother over him. She knew she wouldn't. If she told Griff why herself, could he understand how important it was for Clay and Jeb to remain a family? Even if, with his new perspective, he did, not being able to parent his own child might well drive a thicker wedge between Griff and Clay than she was already sensing was there, which she knew was because of her causing Clay to have to hide something this important from his brother. She couldn't be responsible for their relationship falling apart completely, and she didn't see how it would hold up at all with the news.

And more than all that, she was afraid, just as she'd been years before, that if Griff knew the truth, something would go terribly wrong and she would wind up losing him again—and maybe even Jeb, too.

No matter what she chose, there would be hurt. She could only pray that everyone's life would turn out for the best, and that this time around, her decision would be the right one.

And that was what she told Clay a half hour later back at the farm.

"Are you certain this is what you want?" Clay

asked, keeping his voice low, even though Tessa and he were secluded in Griff's old room away from the guests and family. She would have preferred Clay's old room in which to break off their arrangement, but Mary had designated it a temporary baby and kid rest stop, and it was occupied.

"I think it's the best thing to do. With Griff out of here, there's no chance he can come between you and Jeb."

"Once you marry Griff, even if it doesn't work out, there'll be no turning back to become Jeb's mother. I won't put my son through that."

The two words, "my son," had just a little more emphasis to them than usual.

"You're angry."

"No sense in being angry." He gave a single shake of his head. "I just don't want Jeb to go through any more upheaval. It's been hard enough on us, what with Lindy, and now this."

"I know. But it would be far worse if he had to worry about losing you. Marrying Griff is the only way I can think of to help ensure that never happens."

"That doesn't mean it won't," Clay warned.

"I know. But the odds will be better against Griff ever finding out anything if he's off somewhere far away with me."

Clay's only comment was a slight movement of his jaw. His eyes were filled with doubt—and resignation.

"After you tell Jeb the wedding's off, I plan to tell Griff that the two of us can return to North Carolina as soon as possible." She reached up and patted him awkwardly on the arm. "Clay, thank you for everything."

He seemed to relax. "You and Griff always did belong together. Be happy, Tessa. You deserve it."

"I will be." She would *try* to be, anyway. Tessa wanted Griff, she needed him in her life. She knew she was doing the best thing for Jeb, assuring that he would never be in the middle of a family dispute, or made to move with a father he'd never known.

"You'll find a good mother for Jeb, right?" she asked Clay, feeling a hot flood of tears rise in her eyes. She blinked them back.

He held up both his hands and half smiled down at her. "Oh, no. I'm not answering any questions about that, nor am I making any promises."

The worry that sprung up inside her like a tiny gusher must have reached her face, for he added, "Trust me to be the father you always thought I could be, Tessa. And don't worry so much. Jeb will always have his grandmother in his life. That worked well for you, didn't it?"

It had. The reminder helped; it helped a lot. "What will you say to Jeb? Do you want me to be there?"

"I'll handle it alone, thanks. You go on and talk to Griff. Make your plans, get ready to leave. I'll break it to everyone after you're gone."

She nodded. "Thank you." Much as she wanted to tell Jeb herself, she knew if she did she might not be able to go through with it. This was the best way.

With a quick, sisterly kiss on Clay's cheek, she rushed out of the bedroom and down the stairs, wanting—needing—to put her focus on Griff. She couldn't look back at what she was leaving behind—if she did, she was afraid she would turn around, and all could be lost.

* * *

Griff could sense the difference in Tessa as she approached. Her eyes held purpose; her shoulders were squared back and her chin up. She was ready to tell him something, but whether it was "get out of town" or "I love you" he had no idea.

"C'mon," she said, pulling on his arm until he followed her back toward the barn. Behind them, their departure was noted, loudly.

"This time she's kidnapping him!" Jasper said in a gleeful voice.

"Sadie will be so sorry she missed this," Reba warbled.

"Don't you even think about ruining my picnic, Griff Ledoux," his mother called out.

Griff looked over his shoulder to reply to her that this really wasn't his fault, but Clay was already at her side, tapping her on the shoulder and distracting her.

"He'll take care of your mom," Tessa said. When they reached the other side of the barn, she glanced around to make sure no one was snooping on them, pushed back her bangs and wiped her palms on her skirt, then faced him squarely.

"Yes, I'll marry you."

Griff regarded her warily, not liking the unrelaxed look in her eyes. "That's good, right?"

"Of course!"

"Then why do you look like it isn't?"

Griff was sensing, she knew, her sorrow over locking herself out of Jeb's life. She had to be more careful.

"I just hate the thought of Jeb not having a mama." Oh, Lord, that was so, so true.

"We'll have our own kids. As soon as you want." He slipped his arm around her shoulder.

Taking a deep breath, Tessa desperately tried to pretend Jeb wasn't hers, that she was starting a brand-new life with Griff, but it was as if she was denying a part of her body existed. She had to think of something else.

"And I admit you were right," she said. "I was worried about losing my security. But if Grandma can go off and live for love, I guess I can, too."

Griff felt as if it was almost too good to be true. He hadn't been trying to leave Tessa without a family when he'd gotten Horace to ask Sadie out, but it had worked out for the best.

"So when do we leave?" she asked brightly. "Where are we going after North Carolina?" The questions she was asking reminded her of when she'd been little, and asked the same ones, trying to be brave like her mama had taught her to be. "I guess I'll need to sell the bakery."

Don't look back, her mama had said. Always look forward, to new experiences, new friends, new homes. *We can make a home wherever we are, as long as we remember we love each other.* In her mama's best tradition, that's what she would do with Griff.

"We don't have to leave town right away. We can talk about all that when we're alone. Maybe over dinner tonight?"

"No, let's go, Griff. Let's get started on our new life. I want to see what it is that kept you away all these years. Plus I want you to be doing what makes you happy."

"You make me happy." Griff pulled her close to him, wrapping his arms around her, and she rested her head on his shoulder. He'd gotten his wish. Tessa was marrying him, not his brother. However, the underpinnings of guilt still remained. Had he done the right thing? Was taking her away from everything she held dear—friends, the bakery, and her home—the right thing to do?

Griff hoped so. He sensed something was still bothering Tessa, but he was happy enough about her change of heart to brush the feeling aside. She was just getting used to the idea of leaving the familiar, that was all. As soon as she saw how exciting her new life with him would be, she'd get her mind off Claiborne Landing.

"So you've told Clay the wedding is off?"

She lifted her head to nod up at him. "We both decided that the sooner you and I leave, the easier it will be on him and Jeb, what with the gossips and all. In fact, I was thinking of just driving off tonight and calling your parents and Sadie from the road—"

"*Yipeeyahooee!*"

The yell of total rejoicing that seemed to come from the picnic area was so unlike anything they'd ever heard before, they stared at each other, stunned.

"That sounded like Jeb," Tessa said. She pulled away with a hasty explanation. "Since Clay's not telling anyone yet, we don't want to give anything away."

"Good thing everyone's used to us disappearing together and won't guess."

She glanced up at him and saw the half grin that was back on his face. "Don't get cocky. We aren't married yet."

"I'll wait that long."

She shook her head at him, but she was smiling, too, as they moved around the barn's corner and found Jeb was the center of attention.

His eyes lit up like Fourth of July sparklers when he

saw them. He trotted toward them, followed by Jasper and Miss Reba and the breakfast club, and Jacques and Mary, with a reluctant Clay bringing up the rear.

"So what's this Jeb has been telling us? You and Clay have called off the wedding?" Jacques asked, his face carefully neutral as he pushed back his hair with his hand.

Tessa glanced at Clay, who lifted up his palms. "Jeb got away before I could tell him it was all a secret."

"Heck, Deputy, that's no secret," Jasper said, gazing from Tessa to Clay and back. "Everybody knew it was coming."

A wave of giggles went over the bunch.

"I'm glad the wedding's called off,' Jeb said, "'cause now I don't have to share my dad." He grinned up at Tessa. "But I still like you."

"Thanks." She smiled at him through the pain she felt at having to deny her son. "And I still love you, Jeb."

"No, you *love* Uncle Griff, 'cause you're gonna marry him, right?"

Her mouth dropped open, and she glared at Clay.

Clay shrugged. "Hey, I definitely told him not to tell anyone that part."

"I didn't," Jeb denied, but then Clay pointed to the crowd around them, and his eyes got big. "Uh-oh. Good thing I'm only six, huh?"

Everyone except Tessa and Griff started talking at once, and Griff squeezed Tessa's hand and got everybody's attention. "Good news could never be kept quiet long. It's true. Tessa and I were planning on going quietly off to North Carolina where I'm stationed and getting married."

"Over my dead body!" Mary said, moving forward to hug Tessa.

"It's okay with me," Jeb said cheerfully. "I want Uncle Griff to be happy."

Tessa felt numb. Jeb wanted his uncle Griff to be happy. Not a thought toward her happiness. But then again, why should the little boy think about her? He didn't know the truth. To the child, she was just a family friend. She could go, and he would never realize what he'd lost.

"I want Griff to be happy, too, dear," Mary said, stepping back and surveying them both with a shake of her head. "Which is why they are *not* going to elope. We're having the wedding at a church, and the reception right here afterward, and everyone's invited!"

A cheer went up from the guests.

"That is, if it's okay with you two."

Still overwhelmed from thinking about Jeb, Tessa gazed up at Griff, who slipped his arm around her waist and drew her close. She leaned against him, hoping the love she felt from him would fill the empty spaces in her heart from leaving Jeb and losing Sadie, but desperately worried it wouldn't be enough. She'd felt the same fear years before, when Griff had wanted her to marry him and leave everything that was familiar, a feeling she had begun to hate but felt powerless to change.

"I wouldn't miss it for the world," Griff told his mother.

"Of course it's okay with us," Tessa said, thinking that her voice sounded remote, but deciding she was wrong when she saw Mary beam even more widely and felt Griff give her a loving squeeze of approval.

"Yahoo!" Jasper called out, reminding her that there were still people surrounding both her and Griff. "There's gonna be a wedding after all!"

There was, and it was set for the next Saturday. Tessa coped only because all she really had to do was close down the bakery and the house, and she had Griff's help with those. In Sadie's absence, Mary had been delighted to help with details such as notifying everyone Sadie had originally invited—Tessa had given her Sadie's list—arranging for the church and minister, and talking to Judy, their church organist, about playing "The Wedding March," just in case Sadie didn't get her messages in time to make it back.

That her grandmother might not make it, Tessa thought as she surveyed the bakery's kitchen one final time before officially shutting down the Shady Shoppe, was really bothering her. It was already Thursday, and Sadie hadn't returned any of the voice messages Tessa had left. She wasn't sure her grandmother even knew there was going to be a wedding—and she dearly wanted Sadie to be there.

In fact, she wanted to talk to Sadie anyway. Only her grandmother would understand the pain she was feeling at her realization that her going away meant very little to Jeb, even though her managing to keep his true parentage secret meant everything to the child's life.

She took a deep breath and let it slowly out. Get a grip, she told herself. Jeb was perfectly happy with Clay, and that's how she'd wanted it from the start.

Behind her, she felt a gentle rush of air against her skin, and then she was enveloped in Griff's arms and his lips were kissing her neck, bared by her ponytail. His arms crossed under her breasts and pulled her backward, against the hardness of his body. Closing her eyes, she relaxed and let out a tiny sigh of contentment. Being in his arms seemed so right. Since she'd agreed to marry him that was always her first thought whenever he held her, and then she would stop thinking, and desire would take over.

But she couldn't stop thinking today. Holding her clipboard out to one side, she twisted around until she faced him, trying to ignore how good her breasts felt brushing against his chest. There was just too much to be done. She gave him a kiss on his cheek and then pointed toward the door.

"The Realtor's due any second."

"Okay. I'll stop kissing you when she gets here." He leaned his head down, but she shook her head and ducked out of his arms.

"If I keep kissing you, I won't have my wits about me when I talk to her."

"That's a compliment, isn't it?"

"Yes, it is." Like he didn't know.

"Oh, good."

"Not necessarily. I need my wits about me to get everything ready for our move." Her eyes teased him. "You might not get kissed again until after the wedding."

"That's two whole days!" He plucked the clipboard out of her fingers and put it aside on the counter. By the time she realized what he was planning, she found herself lifted and sitting on the island, with one leg on either side of Griff. "I'm on vacation. I'm not waiting two whole days to have fun."

She giggled. "Okay. I'll just have to fit you in." She studied her watch. "I'm available for kissing at approximately 2:00 p.m. tomorrow. Will that work for you?"

"I'm not clock-watching, either." Leaning forward, he met her lips with his own, and Tessa leaned into him. Yearning quickly overtook her desire to tease him, and she wrapped her arms around his neck and slid forward until her body was flush against his. He deepened the kiss, his tongue slipping in between her parted lips, and she moaned with pleasure. His fingers wound under her T-shirt, caressing the bare skin of her back. For the life of her, she couldn't think of any reason to stop him, so she kept kissing him until she began to forget all her problems and where she was and that she had issued a "no lovemaking until after the ceremony" rule to begin with.

All too soon, he pulled away from her lips, and gave her that lopsided smile that was distinctly Griff's. "Are you witless yet?"

"Extremely," she said, wondering when she had last felt this totally relaxed.

"Any doubts that we're doing the right thing?"

Her eyes met his dark blue ones, and she shook her head. "None. Why?"

"While we've been packing, cleaning, all the other stuff—I've been catching you just staring sometimes, with a sad look on your face. I want to make sure you're not having second thoughts about leaving."

"I'm not," she assured him. Any doubts she had, she was ignoring for the sake of her sanity. "I want to marry you, Griff. I think I always have. I just never thought it could work before."

"You do now?"

She nodded. "You've changed."

"Can someone really change in a week?" he asked. "I still want to fly."

"I think the years you were away changed you and that's why you came here to begin with. You knew the life you had wasn't working for you anymore and you were looking for a life that would."

"I was looking for you," Griff said, brushing a couple of long locks of her ash-blond hair back behind her ear with his fingertips. She covered his hand with her own and tilted her cheek into his palm.

"And you?" he asked. "If you're ready to leave, why the long, sad looks I've been catching?"

"Sadie," she said, amazed at how easily the evasion of truth slipped off her lips. "I've been worried about her not answering my messages. Even if she has a good reason for that, I've been worried she wouldn't get back here in time for the wedding. I don't know if she has a computer available, but I sent her an e-mail this morning just in case her cell phone is messed up." Or lost, or broken.

"We could postpone the wedding," he suggested.

"No!" She pushed him backward and slid off the island onto her feet. "Nothing is going to stop this wedding."

"Good. Now that you've said that I want to give you something." He took a small, velvet box the same color as her eyes out of his jeans' pocket, and presented it to her. For a long moment, all she could do was stare at him.

"A fiancée needs an engagement ring, right?"

She nodded, biting her lips together to hold back her emotion. Flipping open the lid, she stared down at a single diamond on a delicate gold band.

"It's perfect." It was so different than the one she'd already returned to Clay, because she knew as she lifted her gaze to meet Griff's, this ring meant love, promises and everything wonderful that she'd always wanted.

He slipped it onto her finger while she held her breath. It fit as if it had been meant to be. She hugged Griff for dear life, vowing that whatever happened in their future, she would never, never hurt this man. She, Griff and Jeb were all going to live happily ever after, even if it meant being miles apart. She'd see to it. Griff wanted her, she wanted him and this was the best solution for everyone—including their son.

But as soon as those thoughts filled her head, she remembered telling Clay that her and Griff's leaving as soon as possible was the best thing, so they didn't chance having anything else happen and Clay's skepticism about the chances of Griff's not finding out. Griff was still sensing that something was between them—she wasn't hiding it well enough. The same old feeling of impending trouble came over her again, and she tried to shake it off. Everything was settled. Nothing was going to happen. She wouldn't let it.

As Griff watched Tessa go to the door to greet the realtor, he could still feel that wall between them. It was broken down in some places, but not in others, like when he tried to talk about the years after their breakup, or about having children. Then she would

grow remote, and the light would leave her eyes, and
the wall would come up.

He wasn't sure why talking about her past would be
so difficult for her, as from what he'd gleaned from his
parents, she'd lived a pretty quiet life. About kids, she
would only say she wanted a couple, but they could
talk about that later after they had been married a
while. He got the impression she didn't want to discuss
it at all, which he found strange, considering mother-
hood was her reason for wanting to marry Clay in the
first place.

But Griff believed she honestly loved him, and he
knew he loved her, and so he figured the wall would
someday crumble down. He was counting on it, because the fact that the wall existed worried him where
their future happiness was concerned.

It worried him a lot.

Chapter Nine

"It was the strangest thing," Tessa told Griff as they turned onto the driveway on her grandmother's property. "All through the wedding rehearsal, I felt like your eyes were on me."

"They were," he told her, pulling far over to the left next to the house to give Clay, Jeb, Jacques and Mary, who were following in two separate vehicles, plenty of room to park. "I didn't want anyone to kidnap you away from me."

"Like that is going to happen," she said, pausing with her fingers on the door handle. Her eyes met his, twinkling with mirth. "Your mother and father were each guarding a door. No one's going to stop this wedding. Or the honeymoon. Especially not the honeymoon."

"Promise?" Griff asked her, reaching out with one hand to touch the flowing locks of her hair tumbling over her shoulders. She leaned forward and kissed him, her hands clutching his shoulders, her insides aching for what she knew was coming after the wedding.

"I promise." She pulled back and wrinkled her nose teasingly at him. "Though there is that unknown factor, I guess."

"Which would be?"

"One of the other beaus from my past showing up to kidnap me tomorrow."

"That's a possibility, huh?"

She grinned. "You came, didn't you?"

"True. I guess I'll just have to borrow Clay's handcuffs and latch you to me, starting tonight."

"You wouldn't dare!" she said, her laughter filling the truck. It felt so good to tease and be teased. Like the old days before Griff had gone off and everything had changed. For one precious evening, Tessa had been allowing herself to forget the past had ever happened, and basking in Griff's love.

He pushed open the door, and got out, calling out Clay's name. His brother, walking up from where he had parked, Jeb by his side, raised his eyebrows in question.

"I need to borrow your handcuffs," Griff said as Tessa joined him.

"For what, Uncle Griff?" Jeb interjected.

"You don't want to know," Clay told him and shot a pleading look at Tessa.

"Uncle Griff's just teasing, Jeb." Tessa handed the child her door key. "Run on up and unlock my door for me. I have a cake waiting for us as a treat."

"All right!"

With Jeb out of the way, Griff smirked at her. "That's okay. The handcuffs can wait until later."

"What handcuffs?" Mary asked as she approached, hand in hand with Jacques.

"The ones I'm going to use to handcuff Griff to the lamppost out here," Clay retorted. "At least then we'll make sure this wedding happens."

"Oh, this wedding's going to happen," Mary warned, looking at Griff, "if I have to personally escort you and Tessa to a justice of the peace at the point of my knitting needles. And you boys quit that fighting. This is supposed to be a happy time."

"He started it," Griff and Clay both said at once. They all laughed, even, Griff was pleased to see, his brother.

The entire day, Tessa had been almost carefree, and Griff was starting to feel as if maybe the wall had finally come down. He slipped his arm around her waist and guided her toward the stairs leading up to her second floor apartment right behind Clay, who had followed Jeb up.

Griff had already told her she'd never looked more beautiful, and as he pulled her tightly to him, he almost told her again. Her dress was a deep rose that brought out the color in her cheeks, and had some sort of sheer stuff layered over it that flowed when she walked and made him crazy with desire whenever he touched her. As did the low V neckline that stopped, in a tantalizing way, right before her cleavage began, and the row of tiny buttons that seemed to go on forever down the rest of the front. The urge to unbutton them, one by one, to refresh what were only gossamer memories of her body threatened to overwhelm him. It was only hearing Jeb's soft laughter at the top of the stairs as he finally found the right key and worked it into the lock, and his mother's voice behind them, that kept Griff from suggesting to Tessa, then and there, that they forget about their promises of celibacy until tomorrow.

"Could you wear that dress to the wedding?" he asked instead.

"No, silly."

"How about on our wedding night?" he whispered in her ear.

"We'll see," she promised, happiness warming her like a quilt on a chilly winter night. Everything had gone the exact way she'd hoped at the rehearsal, and this time around, she actually felt like a bride. A shaky one, maybe, but a bride—not the fake one she'd felt like when she'd attended the last rehearsal with Clay. And it was a wonderful feeling, knowing she was actually going to marry the man she loved.

Griff stepped to one side so she could enter her apartment first, then waited for his mom to pass, also. Mary beamed her approval. Inside, he joined Tessa, standing in back of her and slipping his arms around her. Tessa leaned backward into him.

"Tessa, you've got messages," Jeb told her, pointing to the rapidly blinking red light on her answering machine.

"Go ahead, hit the button," Tessa said.

Just as she thought, the first two messages were friends calling to wish her happiness and to say they would be at the church for the wedding the next day, teasing her about the short notice. A third message was a wrong number, and Jeb, looking bored, stepped back and around to sit down on the plush sofa that was Tessa's pride and joy, her first real purchase of furniture back when she and Sadie had divided up the house so she could have her own place. Tessa pushed aside wondering how she was going to ship it east—or even what she was going to do about the house—when she heard a familiar voice ring out over the answering machine.

"Hello? Hello? I hate these danged things! I couldn't find my recharger for that dratted cell phone, and then we were out of range or something."

Sadie. Tessa felt a rush of gladness go through her.

"I got your e-mail message, though. We're heading back as we speak for the wedding, darlin', don't you worry about that, and I'll take care of the house and the bakery and all for you. I'm so happy that you finally worked up the nerve to tell Griff about Jeb's really being your and his son and worked everything out between you, so we don't have to hide the truth any longer. I don't mind saying—"

Anything else that Sadie might have said was lost to Tessa as her world began to fall apart. Griff's whole body stiffened and his arms unlocked her; Jeb's small face looked first at her, and then to Clay, and then to Griff. Mary and Jacques looked astonished, and then everyone seemed to freeze into place.

It was Jeb who started everything into motion. He took off running out her door and down the steps. Unable to bear looking at Griff, Tessa began to follow Jeb, her heart breaking for her baby, but she got only as far as the top of the stairwell when Clay's hand caught her arm.

"Trust me to deal with my son," he told her. "You need to talk to Griff."

Slowly she turned and walked back inside the familiarity of her apartment, where Jacques and Mary were standing by Griff. She was glad he had his parents, but seeing them together only made her realize that, once more, she was totally alone.

"Griff, maybe you should spend the night with us," Mary said to him, tugging gently on his sleeve. "Jeb is certain to be really upset."

Griff wasn't paying attention. His eyes were focused on her. They were spitting anger and hurt, emotions Tessa had fully expected to see. What she hadn't expected was to also see sadness in his dark gaze.

"Your parents didn't know Clay and Lindy adopted Jeb, Griff," she said gently, just in case they hadn't already reassured him.

"I never thought they did. No matter how bad a son I was, I know they wouldn't keep that kind of thing from me."

The way she had. Even if true, his words stung. The wall between them was back up, thickening with every passing second so much she doubted that it could ever come down again.

"I guess you two have a lot to talk about," Mary said faintly.

"I'll be by later," Griff told his parents in a stiff voice. Jacques, looking troubled, patted his shoulder and left the room without a word. After a sorrowful glance at Tessa, Mary followed her husband out. Griff walked over and shut the door behind them, then folded his hands over his chest and just stared at her.

"To think," he said finally, "I tried to bribe you away from marrying Clay by offering to give you what he couldn't—our child. And he could." He gave a mock laugh. "You must have found that amusing."

"I'm so sorry, Griff." Her whisper sounded really loud in the otherwise silent room. Her knees shaky, she moved to her overstuffed, russet recliner, a gift from her grandmother, and sank down. Griff still didn't move from where he stood.

"So talk, Tessa," he said, anguish edging his voice. "Finally, please, talk to me."

She did. She told him everything about how, after breaking their engagement, she'd found out she was pregnant; about how she hadn't wanted to give up their baby, but knew from experience how important it was Jeb have two parents in a loving, stable home who would always stay together.

"So you went to Dallas and convinced Lindy and Clay to adopt our baby?" Griff's voice sounded hoarse. "I can't believe Clay agreed."

"Lindy couldn't have children—ever—and she begged Clay, and he caved in. They agreed to move back here so Jeb could be raised around Sadie and your parents—" her voice fell to a whisper "—and me."

And that, Griff thought, hurt worst of all. "You could give Jeb to them, but you couldn't call me?"

Tessa rose and began to pace the far side of the room. She told herself not to cry, but she hurt for Griff, and because she'd made a big mistake. She could see that so plainly—now. Wiping away each tear as it fell, she said, "All you've ever wanted was to see the world and fly planes, Griff. I knew you might come home and marry me, but I was afraid if you did you would resent me and the baby both for getting in the way of your dream."

"You could have called me. Maybe we could have worked something out."

She met his accusatory gaze with an unfaltering one. "Like what, Griff? Marrying you and raising the baby wherever you were stationed? Never having one place to call home? Having to make new friends at the whim of someone else?" She shook her head slowly. "That's no life for a child."

His arms came down to his sides and his eyes narrowed. She took a deep, shaky breath as she paused in back of the recliner and watched him, knowing that no matter how this ended, it wouldn't be the happily ever after she'd thought she had when she woke up that morning.

"So you figured you had no reason to tell me about Jeb. But why not tell me about him when I came and stopped the wedding? I asked you over and over why you were marrying Clay."

"It was a marriage of convenience," she said, her fingers gripping the upholstery for dear life. "I needed to finally be Jeb's mother again. Badly. And Clay reluctantly agreed because Lindy had made him promise not to let Jeb be without a mother for too long and he didn't think he would ever fall in love again. So it seemed best for everyone concerned."

"Until I showed up and wrecked everything."

"No, until you came home and proved to me how much you care about family—both yours and mine—and I realized that I'd fallen in love with you all over again." If she'd ever really fallen out of love with him. "But I didn't want to drive a wedge between you and Clay by telling you about Jeb, or have Jeb's world torn apart in any sort of custody battle. I still don't want that."

"Oh man, Tessa." Griff came around and sat down on the chair farthest from her. His body slumped slightly forward until his forearms rested on his thighs, and his gaze raked her over. "He's my son. You should have told me. Maybe I wouldn't have made a good father back then, but then again, maybe I would have."

"That's a pretty big maybe when it comes to a

child's whole life, Griff," she said, holding her chin up.

"Especially if I'd made the right choices, Tessa," he said evenly, and her gaze dropped away from him. He was right, and she knew it. Damn, but she'd made a mess of everything.

"Regardless," he added, "I should have been given the opportunity to be in Jeb's life from the start, like you were."

She couldn't deny that either.

"I don't know what to do about Jeb," he continued. "I'll have to talk to him, find out what he thinks of all this, so I can figure out what's best for my son." He straightened up, and took a breath. "My son," he repeated quietly, and then shook his head. "This is a disaster."

Tessa wanted to beg him not to try to take Jeb away from Clay, but she didn't. Enough damage had been done for one night, and she was afraid to make matters worse.

He stood, but stayed where he was. "You don't want to leave Jeb, do you?"

"No." She'd never been so sure of anything in her life. "But I do want to be your wife, Griff. It's been tearing me up all week, wanting both you and Jeb in my life."

"I don't know how that could work." His gaze never wavered. "Tess, this changes everything between us. I don't know how I feel now."

"You don't love me anymore because I did the best I could for Jeb?" she asked. Couldn't he try understanding why she'd done what she'd done? Just a little bit?

"It isn't just Jeb," he denied. "It's all the time

you've been accusing me of not being able to give up my dream, and implying how selfish that was, you've been living yours.''

She lifted her chin. "I don't know what you mean."

"Your dream is to always have everything exactly as *you* want it, so no one can ever hurt you again like you were hurt when you were a kid. You broke off our engagement because compromising was out of the question. You decided I shouldn't know about Jeb or have a part in his life. You decided that marrying Clay would let you be a mother again. You decided that you would make sure I left town before anyone could get to me about Jeb—and when I didn't conveniently leave, you decided to marry me and get me out of here—"

"That's not why I wanted to marry you," she protested, but it didn't lessen the hardness of his eyes, the same eyes that had looked at her with such love in the truck not an hour before.

"Okay, maybe you did fall in love with me again. I'll give you that. But it all comes down to you being just as bad as me when it comes to having what makes you feel secure, Tess. We're two selfish people, and Jeb was the one who ended up missing out."

Again, Griff was totally, absolutely correct, and Tessa couldn't say a word.

The phone rang, startling them both. She wasn't sure whether it was a welcome interruption or not, or if there was even anything more to be said between them that could be interrupted. Doubting she could talk to anyone at this point without shedding tears, she let the machine pick it up.

It was Clay. His voice was low, and he sounded the way she felt. Horrible. "Damn, I hate leaving messages like this on answering machines. Look, we're at home…''

With a single look at her, Griff strode over and picked up the phone. He wanted to find out about his son, who was going to become the first priority in his life.

"How is Jeb?'' he asked, shrugging his shoulders to try to work the tension out of them.

"Upset. Tell Tessa he wants to talk to her tomorrow.''

Griff did that, then gave his attention back to Clay.

"I'm surprised you're talking to me,'' his brother said slowly.

"It's not easy,'' Griff admitted. "You could have told me back then, Clay.''

Clay took a minute to answer. "No, I couldn't have. Lindy had just found out she could never have any children of our own when Tessa turned up on our doorstep, pregnant, wanting us to adopt Jeb. I would have done anything to make the woman I loved happy, Griff. *Anything.*''

That was Clay's way of pointing out Griff had failed miserably in that aspect. His shoulders tightened right back up.

"Anyway, we can work out whatever has to be worked out tomorrow.'' Clay paused. "I was really calling to tell you it might be best if you stayed elsewhere tonight instead of coming back here to sleep. Jeb's terrified you're going to take him away from me.''

Hell. Every inch of Griff wanted to slam down the phone, drive over to Clay's and tell his son how happy and proud he was to be his father. Birth father. But Jeb was afraid of him. He wanted to punch something.

"When can I talk to him?"

"Let me see how he is when he wakes up tomorrow morning." Again, Clay hesitated. "*Are* you going to fight for custody, Griff?"

"I'll let you know." He supposed that was rude, but he wasn't in a polite mood. He put the phone down in its cradle and let his hand rest on top of it, as though it was a direct connection to his son. But that was stupid. He had no connection to his son. None. He never had.

"Are you going over there now?" Tessa's soft voice came from behind him.

Griff shook his head, his back to her. He had no urge to turn and look at Tessa. He was afraid of what he might say. But he needed her to know what her silence had caused.

"Jeb's scared of me now. Thinks I might try to take him away from his—" he couldn't say it "—from Clay."

"I'm so sorry, Griff," she told him, her voice filled with such grief that his anger at the situation started to ease out of him. He finally got enough control to turn and look at her.

She was miserable, he could tell by the way she was huddled up in her chair, feet under her, her fingers clenching her skirt. Damn it, he still loved her. He did, but the situation was impossible.

"I've got to go," he said, even though some part of him didn't want to leave her alone. When a tear slid down her cheek, he gritted his jaw. "I have to. If I stay here, I won't think all of this through clearly, and it's too important to mess up."

She nodded. "It is. We both have a lot of things to think over."

Tessa watched him hesitate as though he was about to add something else, but then he abruptly turned and left, walking through the door and shutting it behind him. She couldn't cry at his parting, not with her knowing unlike all the rest of the times someone she'd loved had left her…this time she had no one to blame but herself.

Griff went to his parents' house. They were still up, his father pacing the kitchen and his mother keeping the coffeepot warm. He took a beer instead, hoping alcohol would ease the ache inside of him, but it didn't. Deep down, he'd known it wouldn't, and he let the almost full bottle sit in front of him on the table.

He listened to his mom and dad talk about how wonderful Jeb was, and what a good job Clay and Lindy had done raising him, and he bit back his own thoughts. It wasn't until his mother put her warm hand on his shoulder and told him she was sorry things had worked out this way for him that he even moved, and then only to swig his beer. He was frozen. For the first time in his life, he honestly did not know what the next step in his life would be.

"Tessa has to love Jeb a whole lot, Griff, to give him up the way she did so that he could have the kind of life she'd only dreamed of."

"I would have come back and married her." He gazed down at the brown bottle in front of him, working his lower lip with his teeth.

"Yeah, you would have," Jacques said from across the table, "because I raised my sons to be honorable. But you would have given up everything you'd worked for, and you and Tessa might have ended up fighting over you having to give up the job you loved, and probably over money, too, and the two of you would have been miserable, the way your mom and I were miserable until we finally figured out how to work out our money problems. Did you really want that kind of childhood for Jeb?''

Griff gave his father a long look. He had a point. Not only about how miserable he might have been staying here, but also, had he quit the Academy and come home when Tessa had Jeb, he would have had to serve at least two years active duty as an enlisted airman. He knew some airmen now with families who were struggling with money. ''That's what you two were always fighting about, money?''

His parents nodded simultaneously.

Griff thought back. He'd remembered one time when he'd been little, in the local grocery, when he and Clay had taken ice-cream bars, opened them and eaten half, and his mother had found them and blushed bright red when she didn't have the whole dollar plus change to give the owner of the store. The man had understood and let her pay it later, and his mother had hustled them home, then sat down on the chair outside of the kitchen and cried with frustration. And Tessa had told him of a couple of the times when she'd been a kid that her family had skipped out of a house in the middle of the night because there was no money to pay the rent. He'd known she'd had it hard, but remembering his mother's pain that day made her childhood pain and worry really hit home. He never wanted his child, or a wife, to have to go through something like that—and neither had Tessa. So she'd given Jeb to the two people she knew who weren't struggling, who would love him with all their hearts, and who had promised to live close enough by that she could always be a part of Jeb's life.

He lifted the bottle. "So I understand why she did what she did. That still doesn't give me any answers about what to do about Jeb."

"Oh, in your heart, I think you already know what to do about Jeb," his mother told him, carrying her cold coffee to the sink. "The question is probably more like what you're going to do about Tessa."

And, Griff thought, getting up to drain his beer and throw the bottle into the trash, it was a damned good one.

Chapter Ten

As Griff parked his truck in front of his brother's home the next morning, Tessa was already there, getting out of her car. At the sight of her, deep regret that things had turned out the way they had filled him. But regret was the only reaction to her he was currently allowing himself. If he acknowledged any feelings beyond that, he wouldn't be able to handle what he'd planned.

She stopped midstride, her eyes widening as she gazed at him. She lifted her hands and interlaced her fingers tightly, as though she might be praying—Griff wasn't sure.

"Does Clay know you're coming?" she asked. Her soft, shaky voice and apologetic eyes went into the deep parts of his heart and tugged at his emotions. He steeled himself so he wouldn't bend. But good Lord above, he loved her—and always would.

"No, he doesn't. But I won't be here that long, so I don't think he'll protest."

It ought to have been the cue for Tessa to start up the steps, but she didn't. She stayed where she was, her gaze going back and forth between the house and him.

"You can go inside, Tess," he said, gentling his voice. "I'm not fixin' to yell and scream in there. I wouldn't do that to Jeb." Or to her, he added silently.

She shook her head in denial. "I never thought you would. It's not that."

His trouble was, Griff thought, that no matter what had happened concerning their son, he still cared too much about her. He ought to pass by her, go in himself, get the meeting with his brother and Jeb over with, and leave. But he couldn't, not with Tessa standing there like a doe in headlights.

"What's keeping you from going in?" he asked.

She swallowed, wet her lips and took a deep breath. "I'm a little shook up. The last time I faced Jeb as his mother, he was a newborn. I held him in my arms at the hospital and told him why I was giving him to Clay and Lindy. That it would be the best thing for all of us. And now I'm about to face him again, and tell him I think I made a bad mistake, and that everything he's going through now is my fault, and how sorry I am—" Her voice broke.

"Don't do that," Griff heard himself saying gruffly. "Don't tell Jeb you made a bad mistake. You didn't." Walking to her, he pulled her into his arms and hugged her against him. It felt so good he didn't want to part from her, but he knew he had to. *His son was his first priority,* he repeated silently.

Stepping back, he indicated the front door with a nod of his head. "C'mon. I want you to hear what I have to say to Jeb."

Clay answered the door. Griff thought he didn't look happy to see him, but it didn't matter. Jeb was Griff's blood, and Clay seemed to realize that, because he let him in without a protest.

"Just keep a distance unless Jeb initiates otherwise," was all he said.

That seemed fair. Clay led him into the living room, where the child was on the couch, watching cartoons, and Griff could sense Tessa following behind him, but hanging back, watching. He barely kept himself from glancing back at her, not knowing if she would encourage or discourage him, and not wanting it to be the latter.

"Hey, Jeb," Griff said. He hated the way Jeb gazed up at him, his dark eyes full of suspicion. He should have given anything to avoid that ever happening, but he hadn't, so he stood there and kept his distance while he drank in the sight of his son.

Getting up, Jeb walked over to Clay and slipped underneath the protection of his arm. Clay's hand curled around Jeb's shoulders in a gesture as natural as time.

"He's my dad," Jeb said, pointing up at Clay.

That hurt. Bad. And that made him even more determined to finish what he'd come to do. Griff dropped onto the nearby easy chair.

"I know, Jeb. Clay is your father." He paused for a second, watching Jeb's expression change, ever so slightly, to one of relief. Good. "I just came to tell you that I'm sorry for what happened in the past, but you can be certain I would never take you away from your dad. So please don't worry. In fact, I don't want you to be afraid of that, so I'm still heading back into flying for the Air Force, probably overseas if I can get it. I won't be around much for a few years, and every-

thing's going back to normal for you starting today—"
he took a deep breath "—except that Tessa will be
staying here to be your mom. Please do that for me, at
least—let her. She wants to be your mom so bad."

Jeb looked over to Tessa, then back to Griff, but
didn't respond to Griff's plea. "Do I call you Uncle
Griff, like before?"

"You call me whatever you want, Jeb." He could
do that much for his son; he'd do anything for him,
including letting him have the father he knew and
loved, even if it tore him up inside. "I love you and
your mom, Jeb, and I always will. Please remember
that."

Jeb nodded solemnly. That said, Griff looked up at
Clay. "I'll get my stuff out of my room, and then I'll
be going to Mom and Dad's to say goodbye and leaving from there." Without waiting for an assent, he
headed down the hall.

Clay followed, filling the doorway as Griff finished
packing the last couple of items he hadn't already
packed the day before in preparation for his honeymoon. Griff zipped up his suitcase and straightened,
waiting for Clay to speak.

"Thank you, Griff."

Clay's words were so heartfelt, Griff couldn't be angry with him for keeping Jeb a secret. He understood.
"I would have rather this worked out differently, but
since it didn't, I'm glad you're here for him. Just keep
taking as good care of him as you have been, y'hear?"

"Of course."

Griff could have sworn Clay had tears in his eyes.
But his brother had never cried, not in all the years
he'd been around him, so he doubted he would now.

Good thing, because if he had broken down, Griff would have cried right along with him.

Damn, but he had to get out of here. It would be easier hundreds of miles away for a while, with an ocean between himself and the two people he loved most in the world—Tessa and Jeb. It had to be easier, because he didn't know what would happen to him if it wasn't. Striding out of the room with his suitcase, he didn't look back.

The sound of the front door shutting went right through Tessa, and she winced. Griff was leaving her behind, and she really wanted to go, but her heart and her mind were both telling her not to leave her baby.

Sitting down on the sofa, she reached out her arms for Jeb, praying that he wouldn't run from the room, too. He considered her for a minute with a sad face, then launched himself into her lap. His arms reached around her neck and he held her fiercely, much as she'd seen him hug Lindy before she died. Tessa's eyes clouded up.

"Why didn't you keep me?" Jeb asked against her neck.

The lump of emotion in her throat made it difficult to talk. "I knew I could not give you both a mom and a dad, and I wanted you to have the wonderful childhood I never had. I knew Clay and your mom could give that to you. I gave you up because I loved you so much, Jeb, that I couldn't make any other choice. But please, please don't ever blame Griff for this. He never knew anything about you, and that was my fault."

Jeb pulled back and his eyes regarded her solemnly. "Is this one of those things I'll understand when I get bigger?"

She found herself half smiling, half crying, as she tried not to laugh. "I hope you will, but don't worry if you don't. Even adults don't always understand things sometimes. All you really have to know now is that we all love you so much it hurts."

"Is that why you're crying?"

This time she did laugh. "I'm crying because I always wanted you to have a father *and* a mother, and I'm sad that you don't. But I'm going to stay here in Claiborne Landing instead of marrying Griff and going with him so that I can be your mother. Is that okay?"

"Depends." Jeb climbed off her lap and sat down beside her. "Are you fixin' to marry my dad again?"

He meant Clay. "Oh, no, honey. After all that's happened, I think that would be a bad idea. I'm just hoping to be there for you whenever you need a mom, like at school stuff you do, maybe keep you with me sometimes during the week, and generally take care of you as much as I can." She ought to have talked that over with Clay first, but she didn't think he would mind. She just knew she couldn't have a pretend marriage, to anyone. She loved Griff too much. "What do you think?"

He was quiet for so long her heart began to pick up its beat. She rested her fingers against her chest, trying to calm herself down. Jeb didn't want her. Good Lord, her own baby didn't want her. Her heart twisted.

"Jeb?" she whispered.

"It's okay if you stay. But maybe you should go with Uncle Griff."

She blinked. She hadn't been expecting that. "Why?"

"Uncle Griff doesn't have anybody to love him. He needs you."

That was so true. That was so horribly, miserably true. Griff would be totally alone, probably wary to come back here lest he upset Jeb, and that broke her heart. "But Jeb, you need me, too."

He grinned. "I got my daddy, and he's got me. It's okay if you go. I might even come visit you when I get older. Like next year."

She had to smile back at him at that, but she still wasn't convinced that it was a good thing for her to go. Jeb was so little. He needed a mother's love whether he realized it or not. "Yes, visiting Griff would be wonderful. But that would depend on what your dad says."

"I might find the time to travel in about a half year or so," Clay said from the doorway, startling Tessa. She looked up and met his eyes, but as usual, his face didn't reflect whatever he was thinking. She wondered how long he'd been listening. "I could bring Jeb to visit the two of you, if that's what he wants."

"Told ya!" Jeb said triumphantly. He hurried over to stand by Clay, who scooped him up into his arms, gave him a hug, and then put him back on his feet.

"Go on upstairs and brush your teeth, and we'll get ready to go to grandma's house like I promised."

"Okay!"

Regret that they weren't attending her and Griff's wedding that day instead passed through Tessa, but the feeling left the second Jeb turned and beamed at her. "Love ya, Tessa!" he said, and then flew down the hall to the stairwell.

Her heart jumped with joy. Even though Jeb hadn't called her mom, that was okay. She didn't expect him to. His declaration of love was enough to warm her through and ease up the sick feeling in her heart. Where

Jeb was concerned, maybe, just maybe, everything was going to be okay.

"You can go with Griff, Tessa," Clay said quietly, coming into the room to sit across from her. "I told Jeb you've loved Griff for a long, long time. That your marrying him is the right thing, and always has been."

She searched his eyes, and then it hit her. "You sent the e-mail telling Griff about the wedding, didn't you?"

He nodded slowly. "I was hoping you and he would finally come to your senses and marry each other."

"I thought you believed you and I getting married was a good idea—for Jeb's sake."

He shrugged his shoulders and gave a shake of his head, reminding her of both Jeb—and Griff. "I knew how badly you wanted to be Jeb's mom again, and I kind of felt like I owed it to you to give you that chance because my brother screwed up. I knew Jeb needed a mother, and I have no wish to get into a real relationship. Lindy was enough for me." He paused, gazing down at the floor.

He was still hurting over his wife's death. Tessa's heart went out to him, but there was nothing she could do.

He continued, "But I also knew how much you loved Griff, even if you refused to admit it to anyone. Hell, the whole town knows how much you love Griff. Basically I got cold feet. It wasn't right our getting married, but I didn't want to destroy your dreams. But then I figured if I got you a new dream in the shape of my brother, maybe that would be the right thing to do to fix the mess I got myself into. So I did it."

"Yes, you certainly did," she agreed.

"The question is, what are you going to do now?"

"I'm going to stay here and be with my son," she said, her voice determined. "Even if Griff wanted to stay here and give up flying to be with Jeb, he apparently feels like he needs to be away so Jeb doesn't worry. It just isn't ever going to work out for the two of us, and I've got to accept that and be happy alone. Besides, my staying here and his leaving is what he wants, and for a change I'm going to put his wishes before mine."

Clay stared at her for another long minute. It was a good thing she hadn't married him, she thought, he would have driven her crazy with his stares.

The doorbell rang and Clay practically jumped to his feet. As far as she knew, he wasn't expecting anyone, but she figured he was eager to answer the door so he wouldn't have to deal with her any longer, and she understood that. She could hear laughing at the door, and wished she was someplace else. This was not a happy day for her.

She had a wedding to cancel.

Then, suddenly, Clay was back, with a proclamation that stunned her.

"Looks like," he drawled out, "I'm going to have to kidnap you."

Griff's father was being stoic at his departure, but his mother's face showed every bit of the pain Griff was feeling, and more.

"You promise you'll write?" she asked, sorrow lacing her soft voice. What she really wanted to say, Griff knew, was, "Do you have to go?"

He nodded and patted her shoulder, trying to comfort her. It didn't seem to help. Why should it? He'd been trying to do a lot of things lately, and hadn't been succeeding.

"I promise. And I won't stay away so long this time." He meant that. Even though coming back here would bring him as much pain as it ever had, it would bring him joy, too. He'd made peace with his parents, and he had a son—even if he couldn't exactly claim him to the world. It was a feeling like none other he'd ever experienced.

Except maybe the first time he'd realized he loved Tessa.

But that was over. She had to stay with their son, and even Griff understood how awkward and worrisome his being here would be to Jeb. With a heartfelt sigh that only began to mirror the loneliness he was feeling, he headed toward the door.

"Wait!" Mary said. "You just wait one minute."

Turning, he watched her bolt down the hall and soon, he could hear her footsteps over their heads on the second floor. Griff shot his father a puzzled look and got a bewildered shrug back.

A minute or so later, he got his answer when Mary returned with the cardboard box full of his old toys.

"As long as you are riding through town, drop these off at the Mission Donations box for me."

"It's still in the same place?"

She nodded.

That would make it in the back of the First Faith and Hope Church of Claiborne Landing, which was a small church about a third of a mile down from Tessa's house, but he guessed enough trees blocked the view that he didn't have to worry about the two of them seeing each other again.

"Tessa was talking about saving some of these

things…'' He couldn't complete the sentence, but his mother seemed to know what he was getting at. For Jeb.

"Well, she walked off the other day and left them and I guess it might confuse Jeb to get them now, so I want them out of here," Mary said firmly.

"Okay." He hoisted the box into his arms, leaned over, and kissed his mother goodbye again. Before she could say anything else, he walked toward the door.

"But isn't that where—" he heard Jacques say quietly behind him, only to be hushed by his mother. If he didn't know any better, he would think something was up, but what could that be?

He thought about it the entire five miles to the church, but decided that the shushing had been his mother's softhearted attempt to save him from learning something he didn't want to know. Maybe Clay and Tessa had already decided to go back to their marriage of convenience. The very idea tore him up, but since he didn't know anything for sure, he decided he couldn't worry over idle thoughts.

Bless his mother for finally keeping quiet.

After a left off of Highway 518, he followed the loop driveway around the picturesque church, under the trees, to the back where the big silver canister was kept for people to drop off donations for the needy. He got out and went to the back of his truck bed, where he unhitched the tailgate and slid the box forward.

The second his eyes set on the toys, he had to go through them again, one last time. He didn't know why, just that it was that kind of day. He was leaving everything he loved behind, from his parents and brother, to Jeb…and Tessa. Why not take something familiar with him?

The catcher's mitt reminded him of the ball games his dad took him to, faithfully, even when Jacques had been working in the scorching sun and humidity all day. Funny, he hadn't appreciated back then how much of a sacrifice his dad must have made for him, but now he could. Now, that was, that he'd worked himself as a fully grown man on the roof the week before in the blazing heat, with no pay—not that money was the issue—and been able to do nothing afterward more strenuous than collapsing into an easy chair. His father must have been exhausted, but he'd gone to the games. For his kid.

He put the mitt aside. The fire truck was next. He remembered the year he'd received it, they'd taken a beating on the crops—lousy weather. Very little money, but still there had been presents to open on Christmas.

And finally, the toy planes. His mother had always bought him one whenever she could afford it, just as she'd always listened to his dreams of becoming a pilot. It must have torn her up knowing that meant he would be leaving home, probably never living nearby again, and he'd hated the way she'd tried to get him to farm with his dad instead, but she'd always gotten those planes for him, and admired them when he'd finished putting them together.

As the good memories swept over him and multiplied, the thought of giving away the toys made him sick inside. But he couldn't bring back the past. He had to go on. Still, he couldn't make himself slide the box into the big one beside him. He stood there, feeling like a fool, undecided.

Beep, beep…beep beep beep.

He raised his head to see who was trying so hard to

get his attention, and saw first one vehicle, then another, and another, of assorted makes and colors, coming up the driveway and rounding the church. His mother and father, Sadie and Horace, Jasper and his wife, and others. Once the first of the vehicles was on the other side, they parked between the trees on one side and the church on the other, so that they neatly blocked access out. Two more cars blocked almost all of the driveway coming in, and more came up behind them, until one last vehicle, Clay's truck, threaded through the small lane that was left and totally blocked after that by a last car.

Frowning as he listened to vehicle doors opening and shutting, Griff's attention stayed on Clay's truck. His determined-looking brother was behind the steering wheel, with Tessa next to him, and Jeb by the window. Tessa was biting her bottom lip, which meant she was worried.

What the hell was going on? Then he remembered his father's question to his mother right as he was walking out the door of the farmhouse. *Isn't that where…?*

"Isn't that where what, Dad?" he asked as Mary and Jacques, the only ones of the arrivals who weren't hanging back, approached him. He couldn't blame the others. He figured he was looking pretty irritated about then, even if he had been taking his own sweet time about driving on.

"Where your wedding was supposed to be held." Jacques looked sheepish. "We couldn't have the rehearsal here last night because the rugs were being cleaned, but your mother wanted you two to get married in some place different than…" His words trailed off.

Different than where Tessa and his brother's aborted wedding had been.

"Well, the wedding's off," Griff grumbled, being careful not to look toward the truck where he knew Tessa was, even though he heard the door to it open.

"From what I heard," Clay said, ambling up to stand with their parents, with Jeb beside him, "you two never talked that over between you. Tessa was all for letting you make this decision, because she wants you to be happy and to have your way and she knows that if she's here, you'll feel better about leaving Jeb behind. But me, little brother, I think you're being an idiot walking away from everyone who loves you, but especially walking away from Tessa. So we kidnapped the two of you so you could be together and work it all out."

"That's about the longest speech I've heard out of you in quite a while, Clay," Griff said, feeling off guard.

"I never talk much unless there's something important to be said. Makes people listen to me better that way." Clay crossed his arms over his chest. "I hope it's working with you."

"It is," he said dryly. "I'm an idiot. I was standing here coming to that very conclusion myself."

A slow grin spread across Clay's face. "Then I guess we'll all leave you two alone to reason this out."

A buzz of noisy chatter went up behind him as he headed toward the church doors and the group of friends and family followed, but the only thing Griff wanted to hear was what Tessa had to say.

What was she going to say to him? Tessa leaned back against Clay's truck and took deep, even breaths. She watched as he waited until everyone but the two of them had gone inside, and then walked over to join her by the truck. With that lopsided grin that she loved, he settled next to her, assuming her same stance, arms crossed over chest, back against the truck door, hip against her. She didn't mind that part at all. He didn't mind being close. That was good.

"Did they really kidnap you?"

She offered him a tentative smile. "I never go anyplace I don't really want to go, Griff. You know that."

"Yeah, I guess I do." Shifting his gaze away from her, he said, "Mom got me to come here by having me drop off those old toys in my room."

Tessa gazed with horrified eyes over at the big silver box as if it was a steel monster that had eaten a small child's toys.

Griff caught her expression. "Don't worry, I didn't put them in there. I was just standing there, staring at them, wondering how I screwed up my life so badly that I was fixing to leave everything that means anything at all to me behind. Namely you."

"Griff, I talked to Jeb, and you don't have to leave me behind," she said in a rush, hating to see him hurting and wanting desperately to reassure him. "I'll go with you. I want to, and Jeb wants me to."

Bewilderment covered his features. "He said that?"

She told him of the conversation she'd had with their child after Griff had left Clay's house. "He told me he has Clay, and he was sad because he wanted you to have someone to love, too." She paused. "By giving up all claim to Jeb so he wouldn't have to be afraid, I realized you were putting Jeb and me first. I adore you, and so how could I do less? Wherever you need to go, Griff, I want to be with you. And I promise I'll be happy, as long as we can come back to visit on a reg-

ular basis. I trust Clay to take care of Jeb, just as you
were trusting him when you drove away.''

He slipped his arm around her shoulders, unable to
say a word.

''I was so afraid you'd be gone by the time we got
here, and I'd have missed my chance to be with you
again.''

He stared at her intensely. ''That's why I was standing here for so long instead of dumping my past into
that box and leaving. I was thinking that I didn't want
to leave. I can fly anywhere, but I can't have a life just
anywhere. Not one with great memories, the kind that
are keepers—like the ones I had here since I came
back. All the time I was working with you at the bakery, and with Dad on the roof, or watching you with
Jeb—our son—in the pool, it wasn't the agony I remembered. It was wonderful. I felt like I was part of
something really special, and I haven't felt that in
years.''

''Part of your family,'' Tessa said simply.

''That's right.'' He nodded in agreement. ''A family
with you in it.''

''Oh, Griff,''

''I can't envision one without you, Tessa. When I
was thinking about the toys, and remembering baseball
games with Dad, I wondered what it would be like to
go to one with you and our kids. When I was remembering waking up on Christmas morning and seeing
Dad next to Mom on the couch, I knew I wanted you
next to me on Christmas morning, watching our kids
unwrap gifts.'' He shook his head. ''I can't have a life
without you, nor without being close to those we
love.''

Her heart was beating thunderously, and she was almost afraid to ask. "Does that mean we're staying here?"

"Only if Jeb doesn't mind, and only if you'll walk into that church with me and marry me right now."

"We'll have to ask Jeb, but I'll be happy to marry you this very minute, only…what about flying?"

"My hitch is up. What would you think about me processing out of the Air Force and opening up a flying school right here as soon as we can get the cash together?"

"I would love it!" She took his hand and they walked to the church to ask their son the most important question Tessa thought they would ever ask him. If Griff's staying would be okay with him. And to their delight…

Jeb said yes.

Once that happened, Tessa and Griff were whisked off to small, separate Sunday school rooms, Tessa to dress in the gown Mary had brought and Griff in the suit Clay provided since Griff hadn't brought any dress clothes with him. Then Sadie played "The Wedding March" and Tessa came down the aisle on Griff's arm, because he wasn't going to let her get away again. Before she knew it, Griff was kissing her, and they were being presented to the congregation as man and wife.

The breakfast club, for once, was amazingly silent.

Sadie cried with happiness, and Reba and Claudette sighed over the romance of it all.

The congregation cheered.

And Tessa finally had everything she'd ever dreamed of—an extended family, her son, and the man of her dreams.

Epilogue

One year later...

"**M**om's trying to match Clay up with one of her friend's daughters," Griff told Tessa in an attempt to get her off the subject of where they were going. Having dropped their three-month-old daughter, Sherrie, off with his parents, they were driving down the parish highway toward Minden and the anniversary present Griff had to show her, which was supposed to be a surprise.

"Matchmaking Clay? Now she knows that will never work. I've ruined Clay toward getting involved with any woman."

"What?" Griff glanced swiftly at her, taken totally by surprise. "Did Clay tell you that?"

"Of course not." Tessa loosened her fingers from where they were snugly resting in Griff's free hand. "Sadie did."

Griff thought about that for a minute. "Hmm. If it came from Sadie the Sage, it's probably true. Maybe we ought to put some serious thought into making it up to him."

"Help find him a wife, you mean?" she asked hopefully.

"I mean, send him a ticket for a vacation in Alaska. Think that's far enough away from Mom's schemes?"

"Probably not." Tessa giggled, but then her mind went right back to what was really important at the moment. "So what exactly is my anniversary gift?" She snuggled closer to him.

"Now, you know I can't tell you."

"Won't," she contradicted. But she could fix that. After their wedding, she'd quickly discovered she could make him tell her anything. With a crafty smile, she snuggled up to him and skimmed her fingernails lightly up and down his thigh, closer and closer to—

"Stop that or I'll shift you over to the passenger side. Why did they go and make seat belts in the middle of these bench seats, anyway?"

"Your mouth is grumbling, but your lips are grinning." She loved it when he teased her. Heck, there weren't a whole lot of things about him she didn't love.

Her roving fingers were reaching under his waistband, and he caught his breath as he reacted to her in a very masculine way. "Okay, I'll shut up," he told her. "But you'd better stop, or we won't get there."

"Where?" she asked, having brought him right back to where she wanted him.

"Right here," he said, signaling to make a right turn down a graveled, tree studded lane. Tessa watched to each side and saw nothing but green—pines, trees, grass. He drove up the gradual slope about a quarter of a mile and parked at the side of a double-story farm-house at the top of a hill. The view of the tree blanketed valley with a pond carved out in the middle was se-renity and blissfulness rolled into one, and Tessa stared in wonder.

She slipped from the truck and followed Griff inside, up the long staircase, to the master bedroom that over-looked the view. After that they checked out the kitchen and the closets—everything they could see—and ended up back outside. She followed Griff around the house to gaze down at what he told her was a five-acre pond and the forest that seemed to be all around them, tamed in some areas, untamed in others.

"One hundred acres and the house. I figure what with Jeb visiting us a lot, and with Sherrie now, and maybe more kids later, we need more room than just the top of Sadie's house." They'd kept the bottom free for when Sadie visited home. "The only thing is, I know how you feel about having security, and even though the flight school's doing well, the down pay-ment will just about wipe out the savings we have left."

"No, it won't," Tessa said. It was time for her an-niversary surprise to Griff. "Horace bought out my half of the bakery." After their wedding, Tessa had taken the For Sale sign off of it and reopened for business. While she was pregnant, she'd hired Miss Reba to help her. "Sadie's tired of traveling. She says she's missing all the fun of having another grandbaby and being in the middle of everything. She and Horace are going to run the place now with Miss Reba's help."

His eyes lit up. "So you think this could be a place for us to grow old in?"

"I definitely do. I love it," she said with delight. "It's perfect."

Griff gave her an odd look. "The porch swing is rusty, the outside could use a paint job and you said yourself the carpeting will need to be replaced throughout the downstairs."

"And soon it will be filled with the kids—and lots of love. A home of my own, with you and our family in it." She paused, her face glowing as she gazed up at him. "As I said, perfect."

Griff couldn't help but agree.

* * * * *

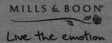

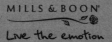

MILLS & BOON®

Live the emotion

Modern Romance™

THE ITALIAN PRINCE'S PROPOSAL by Susan Stephens

Crown Prince Alessandro Bussoni Ferara needs to make a purely practical marriage — and he's found the perfect bride! Emily Weston agrees to the Prince's proposal to help her sister — but once Alessandro's wedding ring is on her finger there are surprises in store.

THE BILLIONAIRE'S PREGNANT MISTRESS
by Lucy Monroe

When Greek billionaire Dimitri Petronides is forced to give up his beautiful mistress he's certain Xandra won't be too distraught. For all their intense passion she has never let him into her heart. But after the split Dimitri discovers that Xandra is not who he thought she was…

A CONVENIENT WIFE by Sara Wood

Millionaire Blake Bellamie has just discovered he's not the legitimate heir to the grand estate which means everything to him. Nicole Vaseux is the rightful owner, and the attraction between them is instant. Only after accepting Blake's marriage proposal does she discover the truth…

THAT MADDENING MAN by Debrah Morris

Ellin Bennet has a daughter to raise and a career to save — finding a man is not at the top of her To-Do list. Bachelor Jack Madden is perfectly content with his life — until he meets Ellin. Now all he has to do is get Ellin to believe he is ready to settle down…

On sale 5th December 2003

Available at most branches of WHSmith, Tesco, Martins, Borders, Eason, Sainsbury's and all good paperback bookshops.

1103/01b

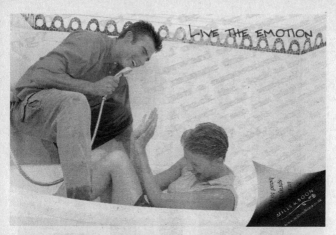

MILLS & BOON®

BETTY NEELS

THE CHRISTMAS COLLECTION

On sale 5th December 2003

*Available at most branches of WH Smith, Tesco, Martins, Borders,
Eason, Sainsbury's and all good paperback bookshops.*

4 Books
and a surprise gift!

We would like to take this opportunity to thank you for reading this Mills & Boon® book by offering you the chance to take FOUR more specially selected titles from the Modern Romance™ series absolutely FREE! We're also making this offer to introduce you to the benefits of the Reader Service™—

★ FREE home delivery
★ FREE gifts and competitions
★ FREE monthly Newsletter
★ Books available before they're in the shops
★ Exclusive Reader Service discount

Accepting these FREE books and gift places you under no obligation to buy; you may cancel at any time, even after receiving your free shipment. Simply complete your details below and return the entire page to the address below. **You don't even need a stamp!**

YES! Please send me 4 free Modern Romance books and a surprise gift. I understand that unless you hear from me, I will receive 6 superb new titles every month for just £2.60 each, postage and packing free. I am under no obligation to purchase any books and may cancel my subscription at any time. The free books and gift will be mine to keep in any case.

P3ZEF

Ms/Mrs/Miss/Mr ....Initials...
BLOCK CAPITALS PLEASE

Surname...

Address...

....

....Postcode ....

Send this whole page to:
UK: The Reader Service, FREEPOST CN81, Croydon, CR9 3WZ
EIRE: The Reader Service, PO Box 4546, Kilcock, County Kildare (stamp required)

Offer not valid to current Reader Service subscribers to this series. We reserve the right to refuse an application and applicants must be aged 18 years or over. Only one application per household. Terms and prices subject to change without notice. Offer expires 27th February 2004. As a result of this application, you may receive offers from Harlequin Mills & Boon and other carefully selected companies. If you would prefer not to share in this opportunity please write to The Data Manager at the address above.

Mills & Boon® is a registered trademark owned by Harlequin Mills & Boon Limited.
Modern Romance™ is being used as a trademark.